Goldilocks

AND THE THREE BEARS

ROBERT SOUTHEY

Once upon a time there were three bears who lived in a cottage in the woods. . . a great big father bear, a middle-sized mother bear and a little, tiny baby bear.

Each of the bears had a bowl for porridge. There was a great big bowl, a middle-sized bowl and a little, tiny bowl.

Each of the bears had a comfortable chair to sit in. There was a great big chair, a middle-sized chair and a little, tiny chair.

And each of the bears had a warm bed to sleep in. There was a great big bed, a middle-sized bed and a little, tiny bed.

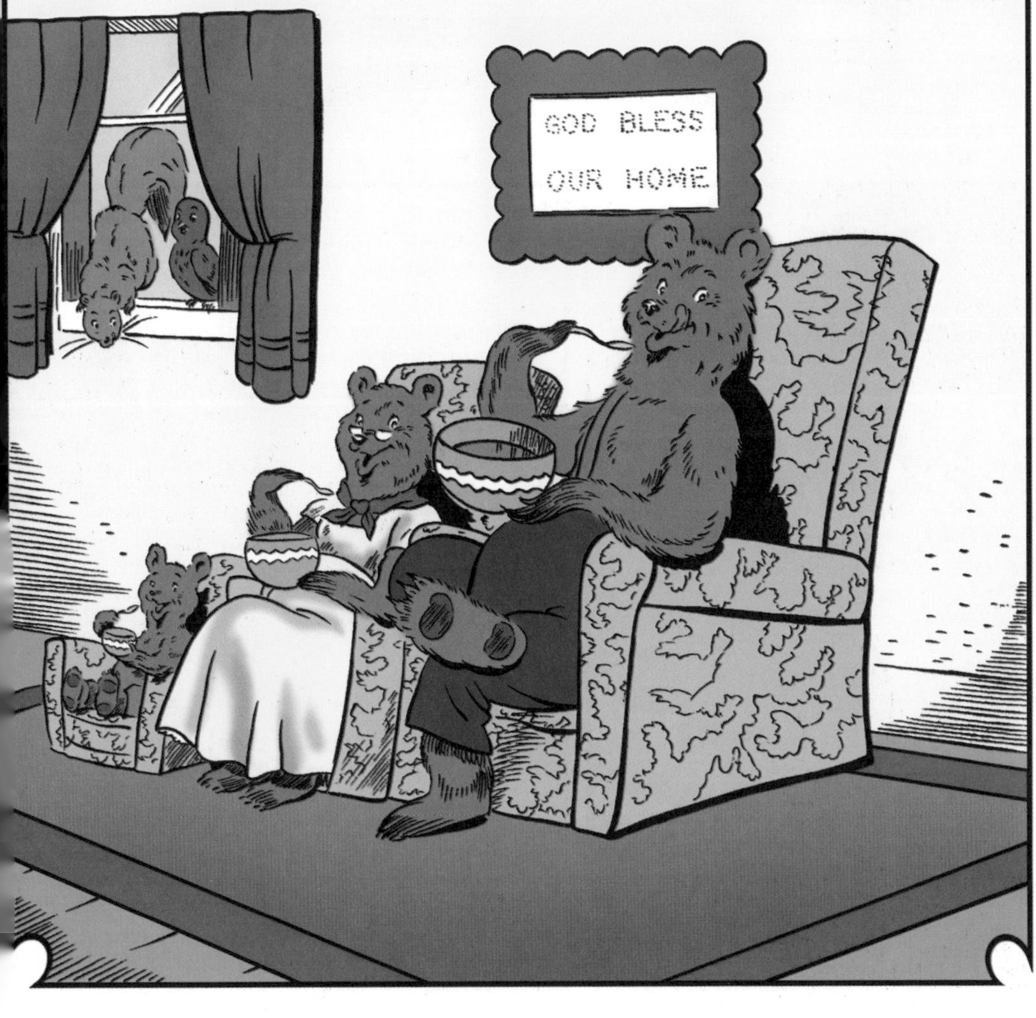
GOD BLESS
OUR HOME

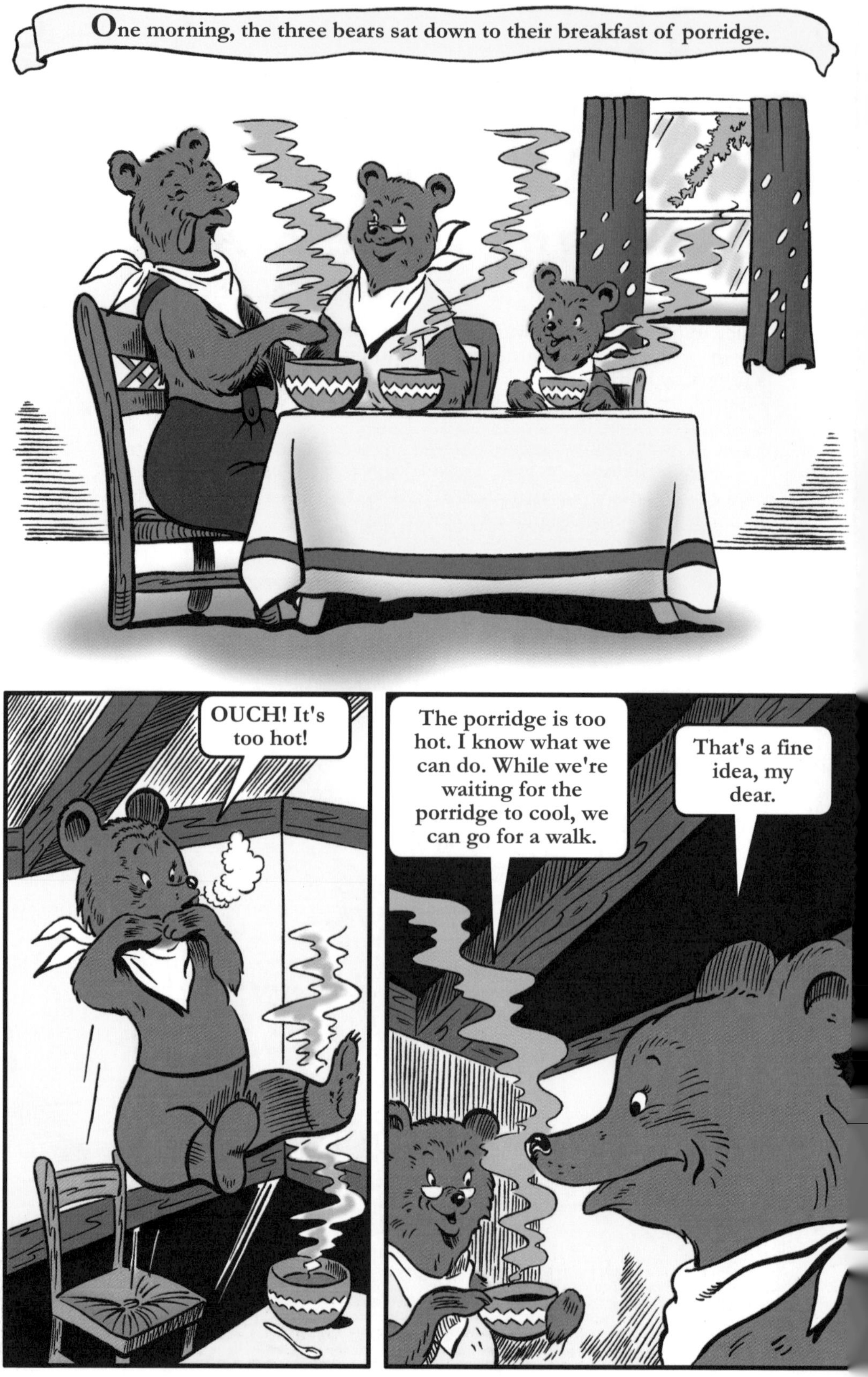
One morning, the three bears sat down to their breakfast of porridge.
OUCH! It's too hot!
The porridge is too hot. I know what we can do. While we're waiting for the porridge to cool, we can go for a walk.
That's a fine idea, my dear.

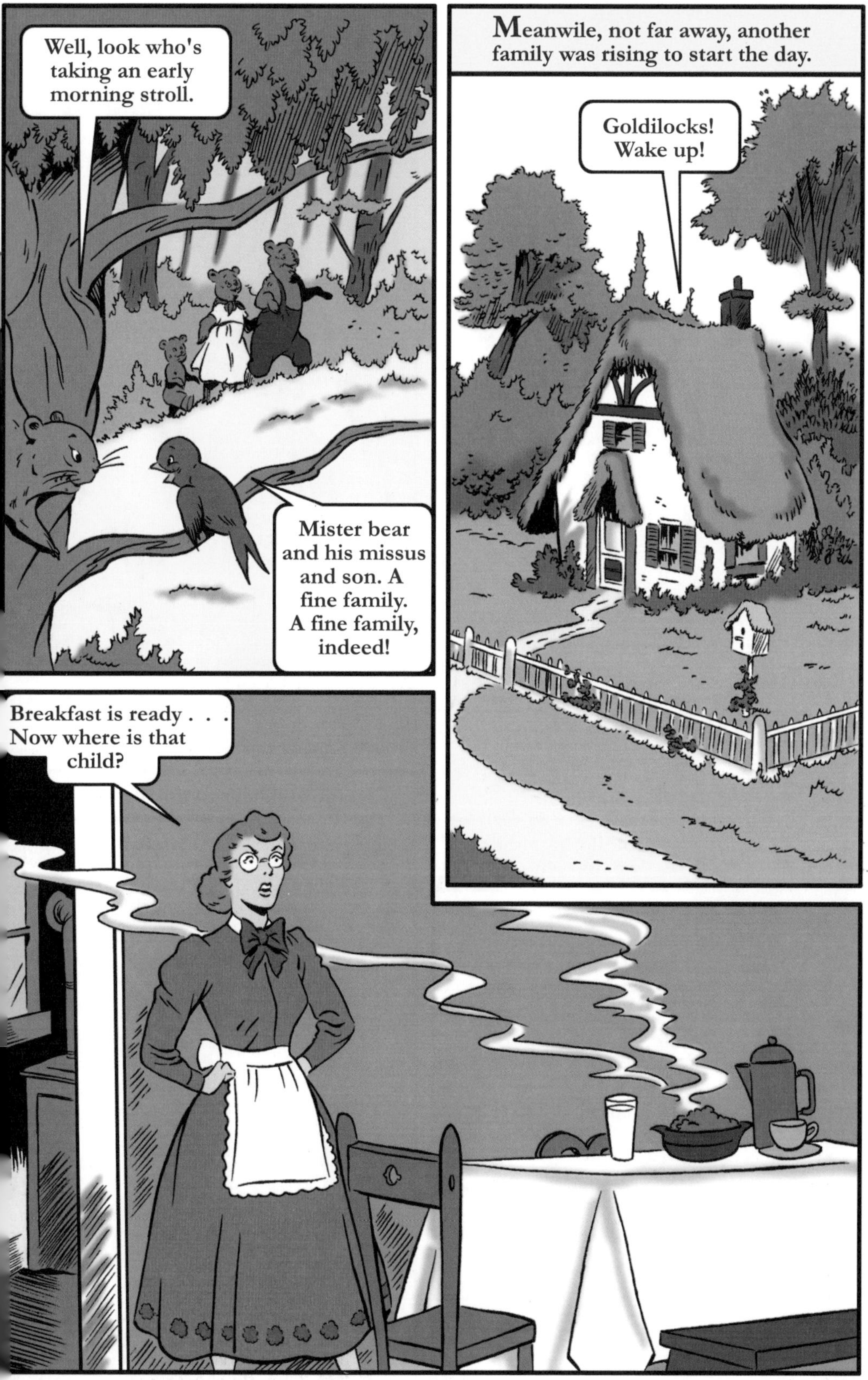
Well, look who's taking an early morning stroll.
Mister bear and his missus and son. A fine family. A fine family, indeed!
Meanwile, not far away, another family was rising to start the day.
Goldilocks! Wake up!
Breakfast is ready . . . Now where is that child?

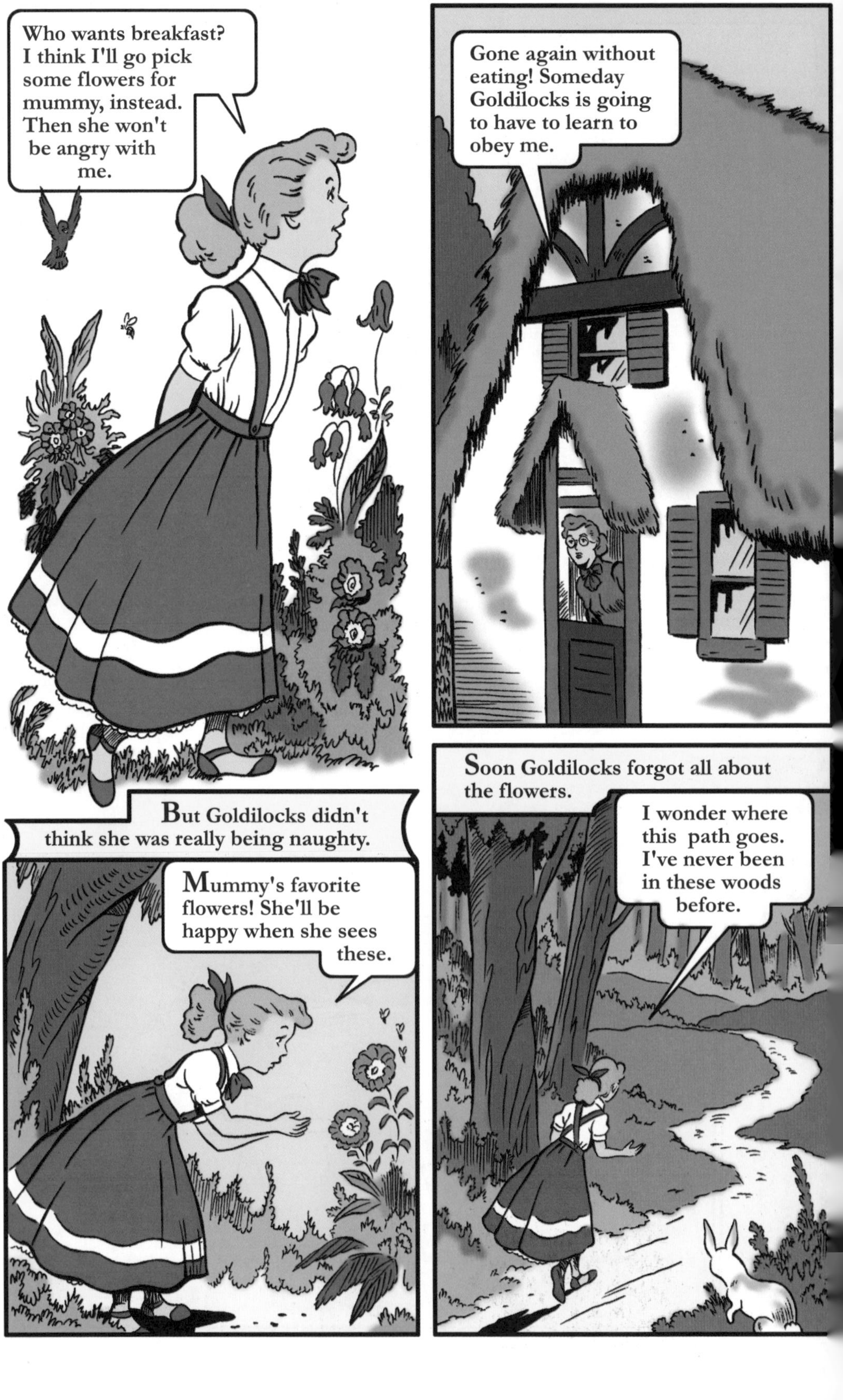
Who wants breakfast? I think I'll go pick some flowers for mummy, instead. Then she won't be angry with me.
Gone again without eating! Someday Goldilocks is going to have to learn to obey me.
But Goldilocks didn't think she was really being naughty.
Mummy's favorite flowers! She'll be happy when she sees these.
Soon Goldilocks forgot all about the flowers.
I wonder where this path goes. I've never been in these woods before.

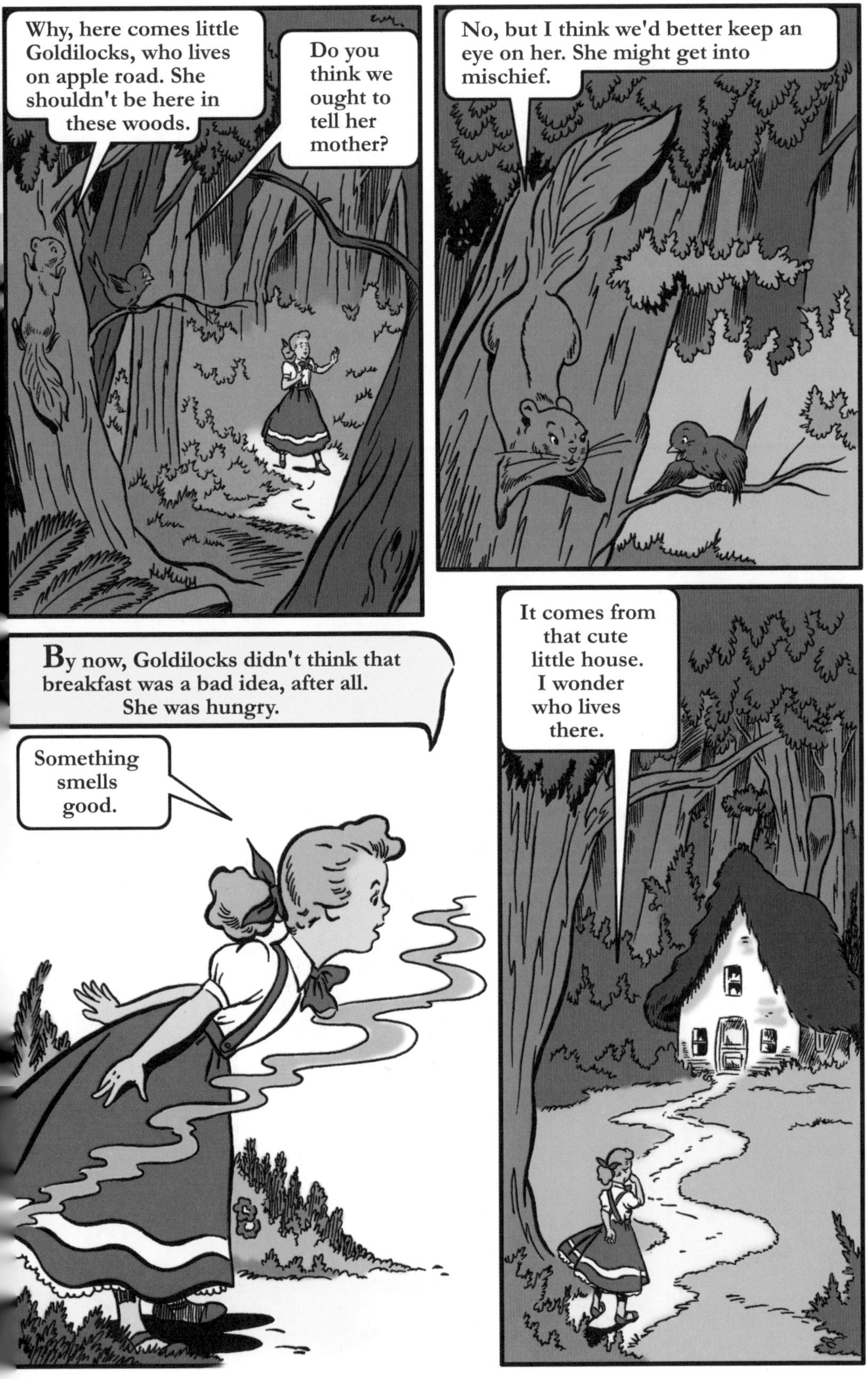
Why, here comes little Goldilocks, who lives on apple road. She shouldn't be here in these woods.
Do you think we ought to tell her mother?
No, but I think we'd better keep an eye on her. She might get into mischief.
By now, Goldilocks didn't think that breakfast was a bad idea, after all. She was hungry.
Something smells good.
It comes from that cute little house. I wonder who lives there.

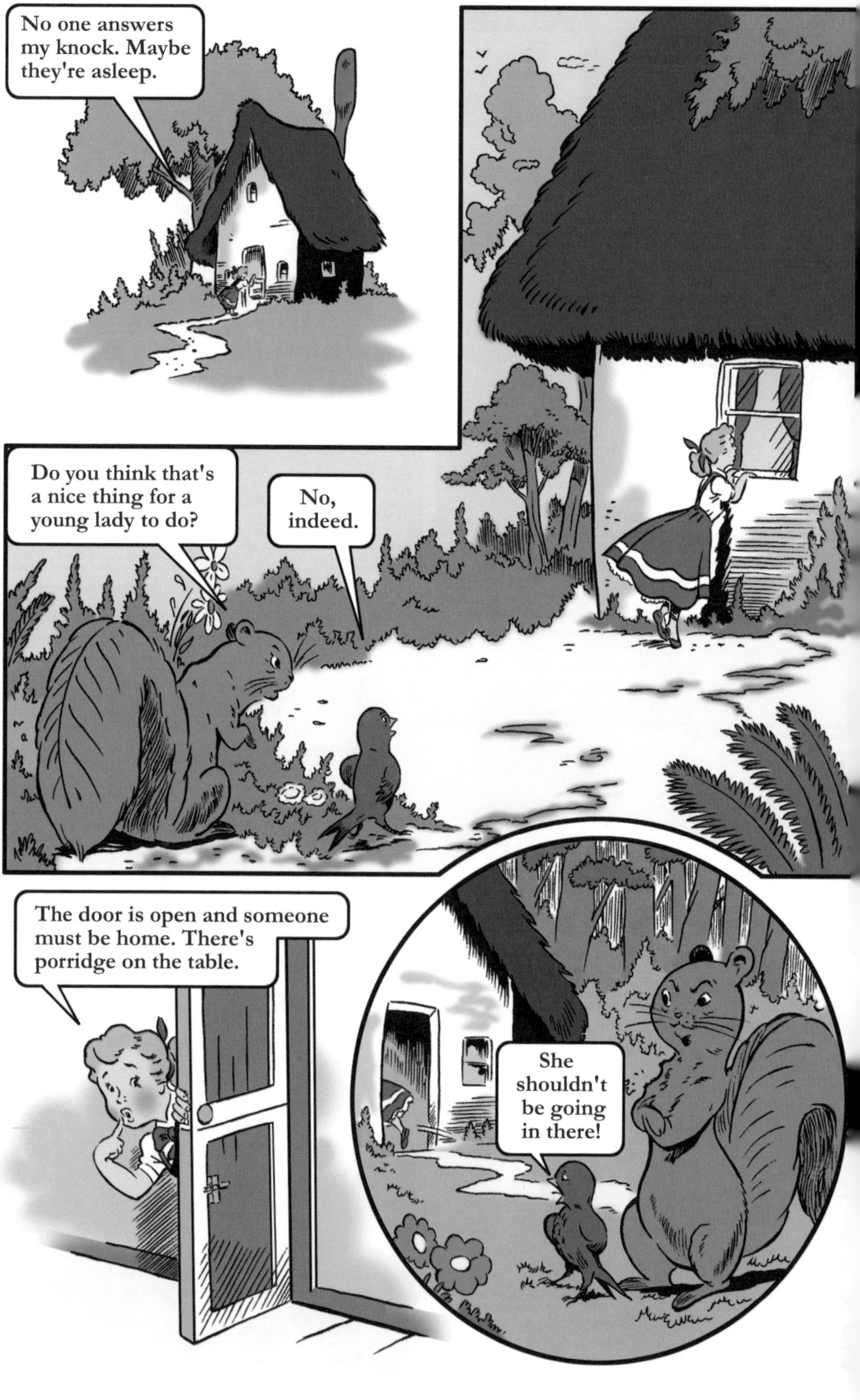
No one answers my knock. Maybe they're asleep.
Do you think that's a nice thing for a young lady to do?
No, indeed.
The door is open and someone must be home. There's porridge on the table.
She shouldn't be going in there!

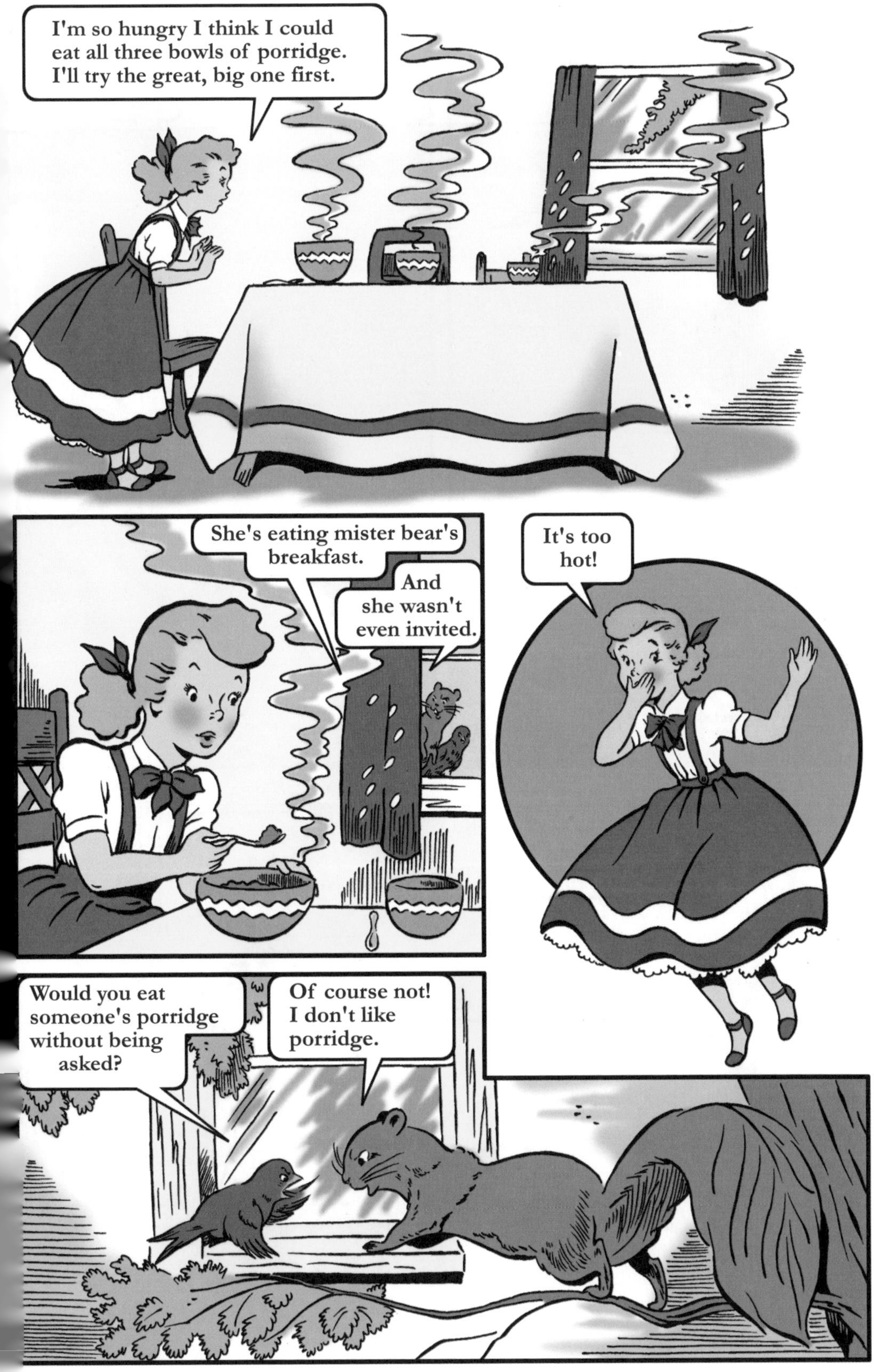
I'm so hungry I think I could eat all three bowls of porridge. I'll try the great, big one first.
She's eating mister bear's breakfast.
And she wasn't even invited.
It's too hot!
Would you eat someone's porridge without being asked?
Of course not! I don't like porridge.

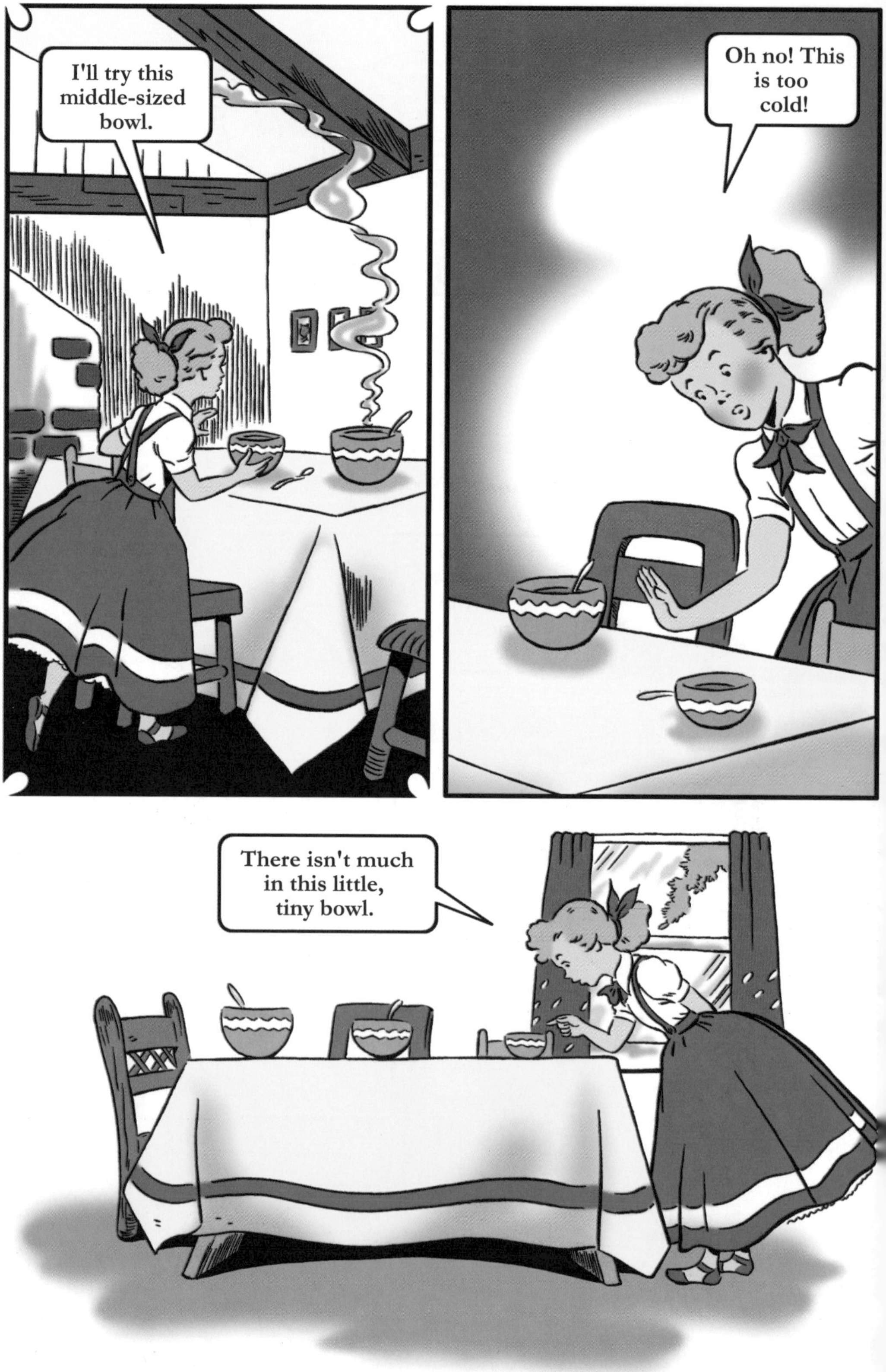
I'll try this middle-sized bowl.
Oh no! This is too cold!
There isn't much in this little, tiny bowl.

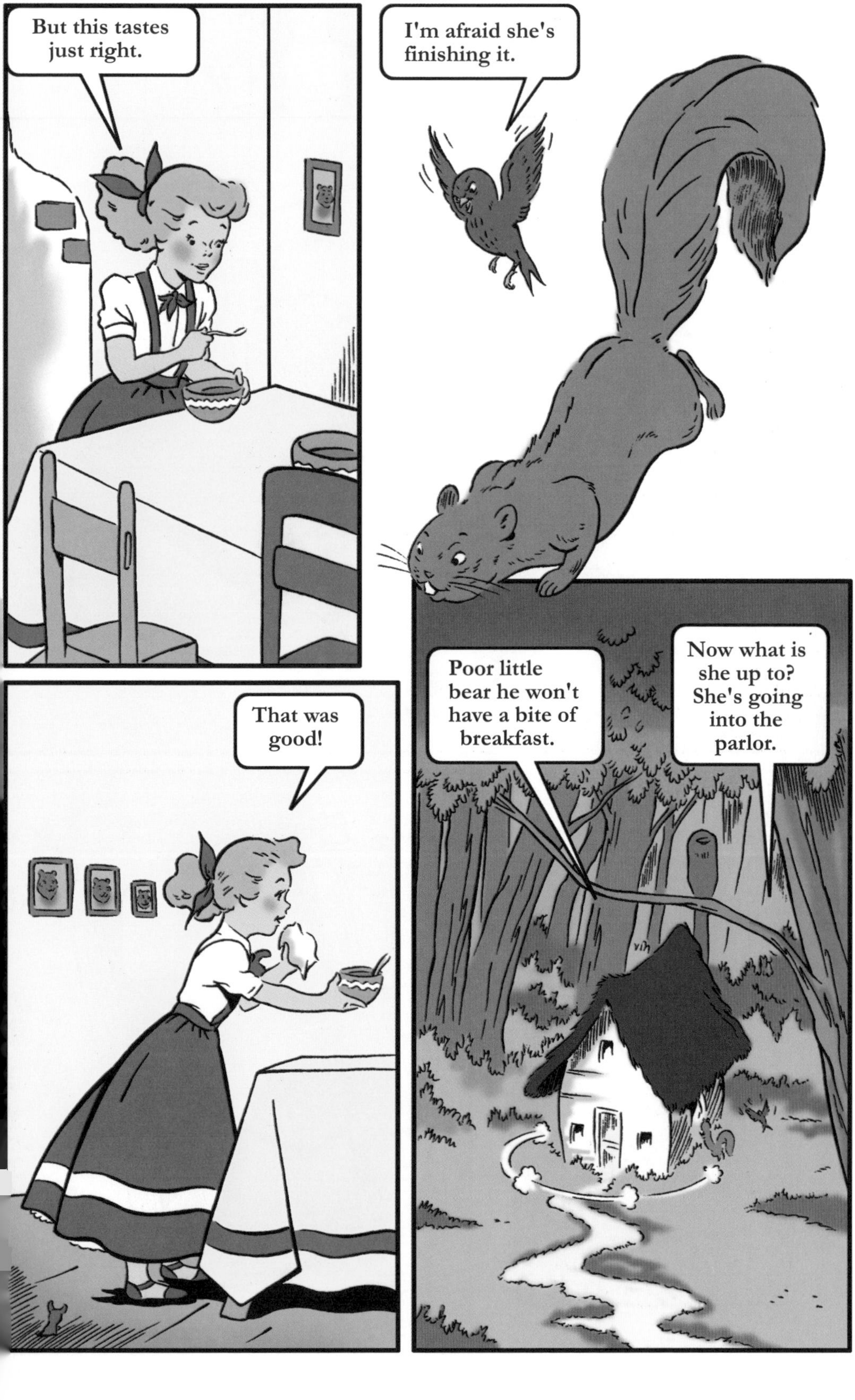
But this tastes just right.
I'm afraid she's finishing it.
That was good!
Poor little bear he won't have a bite of breakfast.
Now what is she up to? She's going into the parlor.

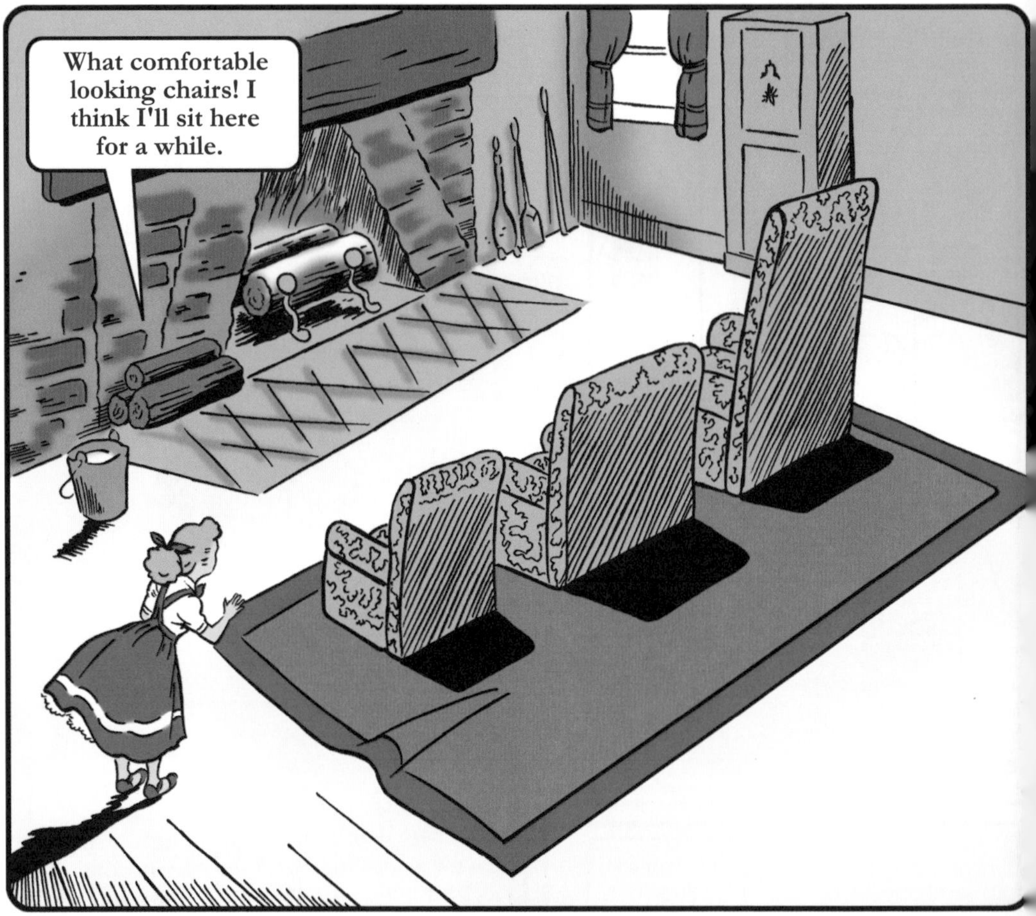
What comfortable looking chairs! I think I'll sit here for a while.

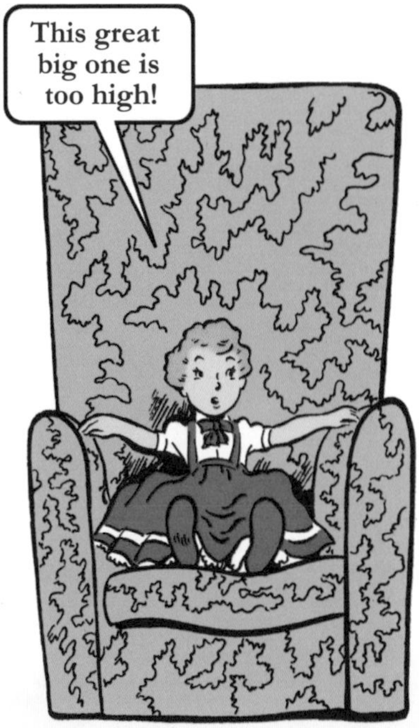
This great big one is too high!

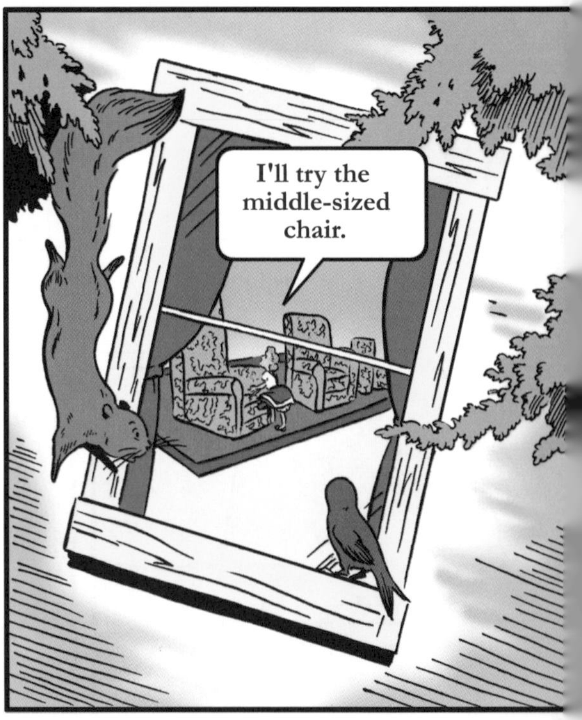
I'll try the middle-sized chair.

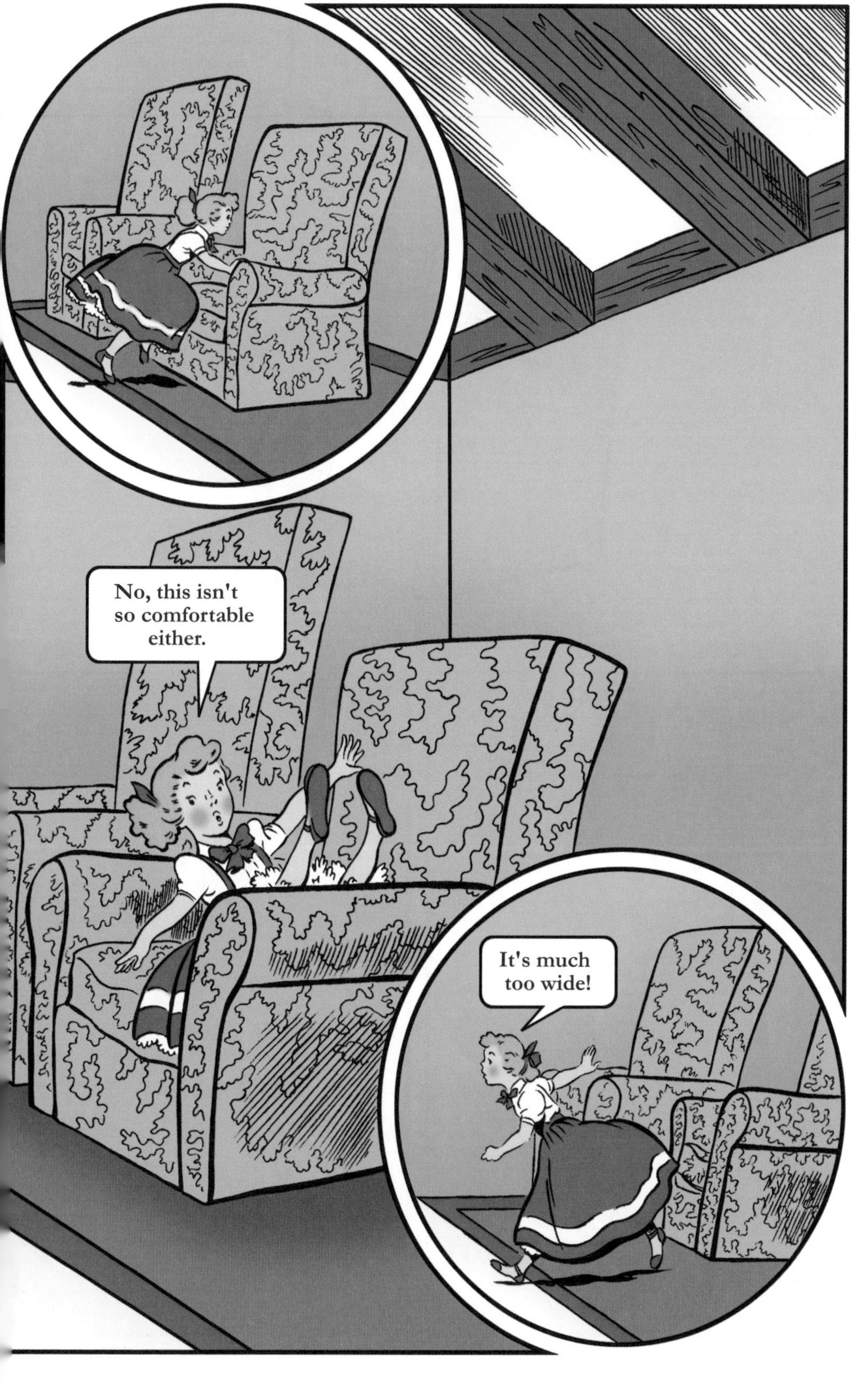
No, this isn't so comfortable either.
It's much too wide!

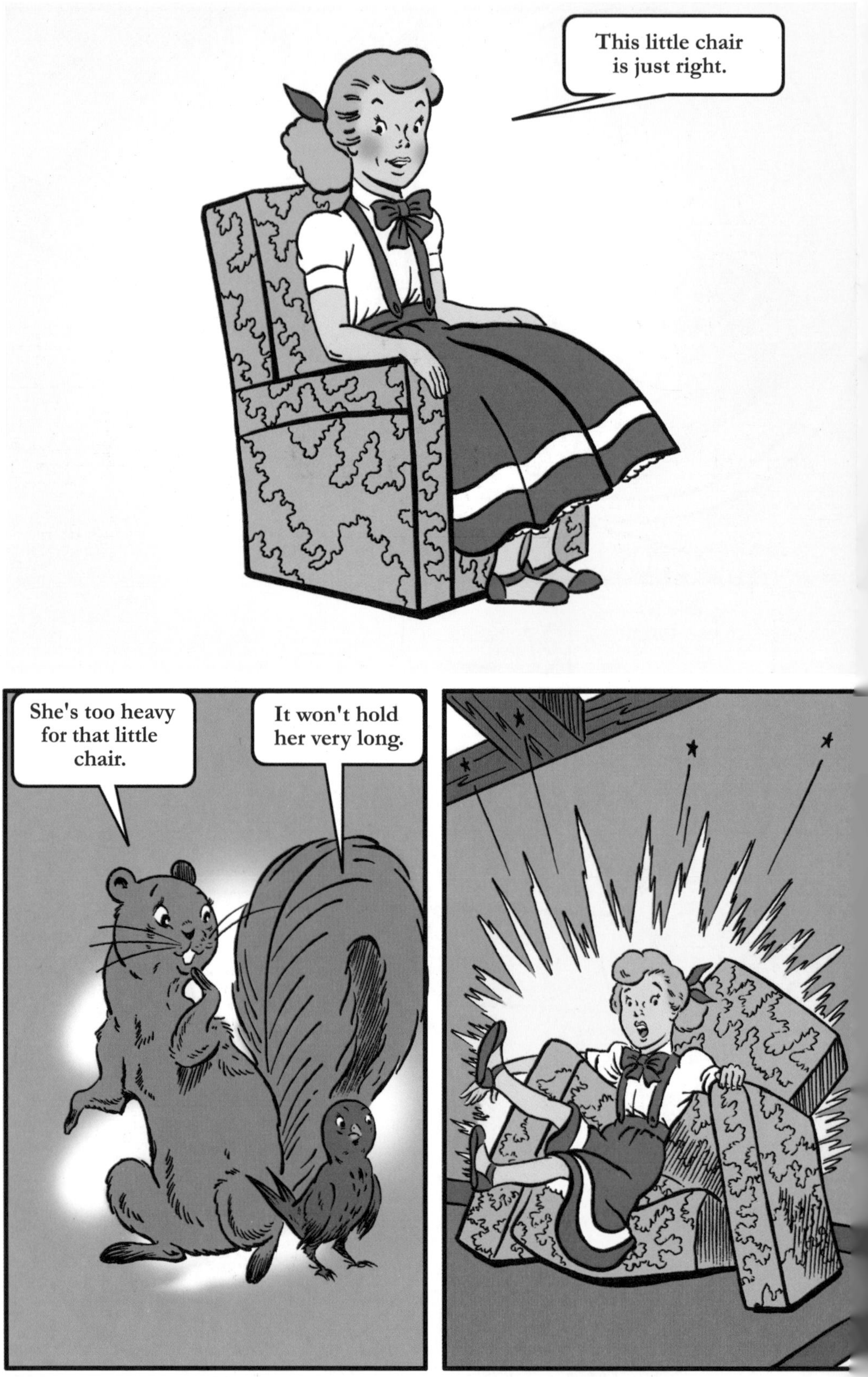
This little chair is just right.
She's too heavy for that little chair.
It won't hold her very long.

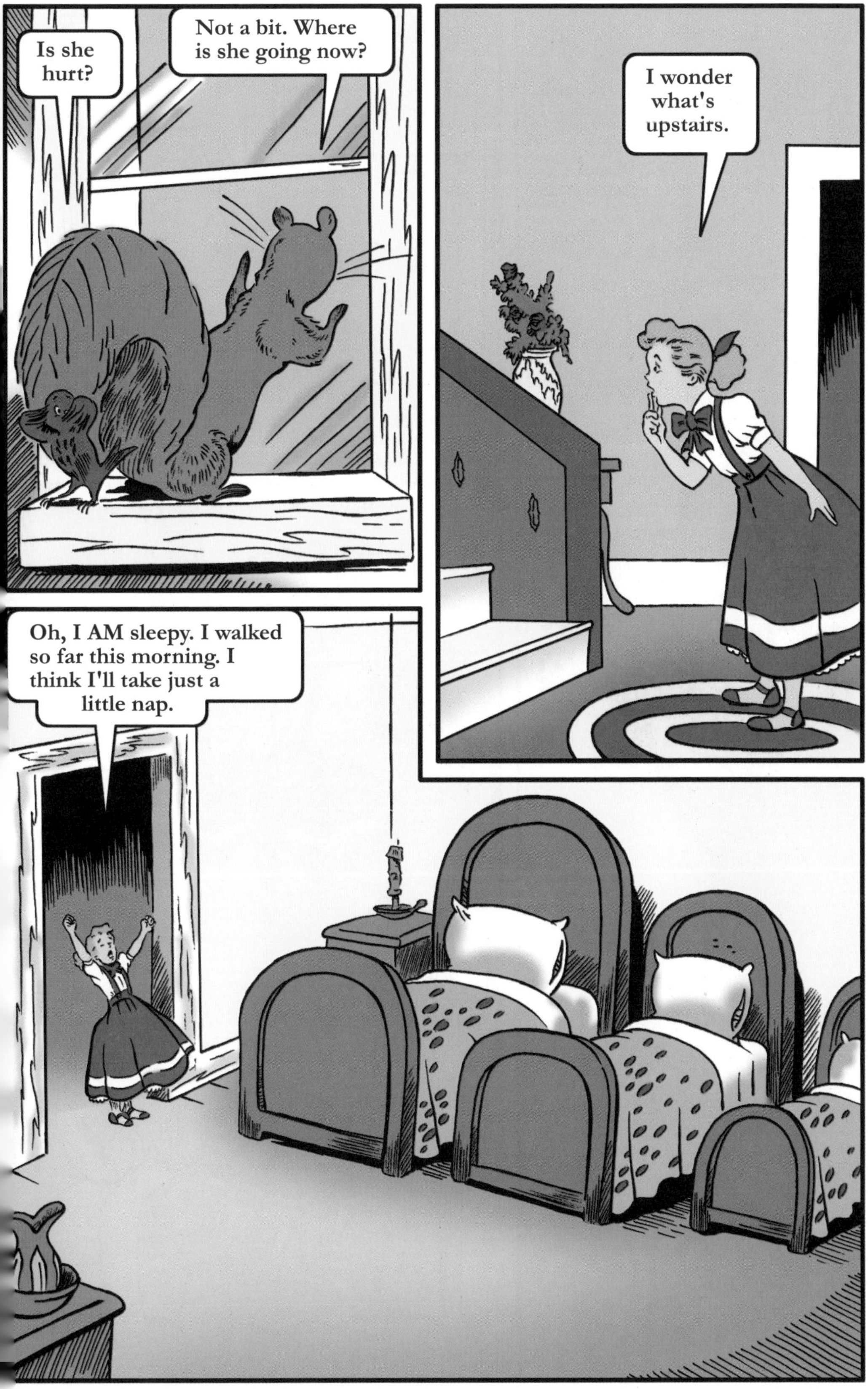
Is she hurt?
Not a bit. Where is she going now?
I wonder what's upstairs.
Oh, I AM sleepy. I walked so far this morning. I think I'll take just a little nap.

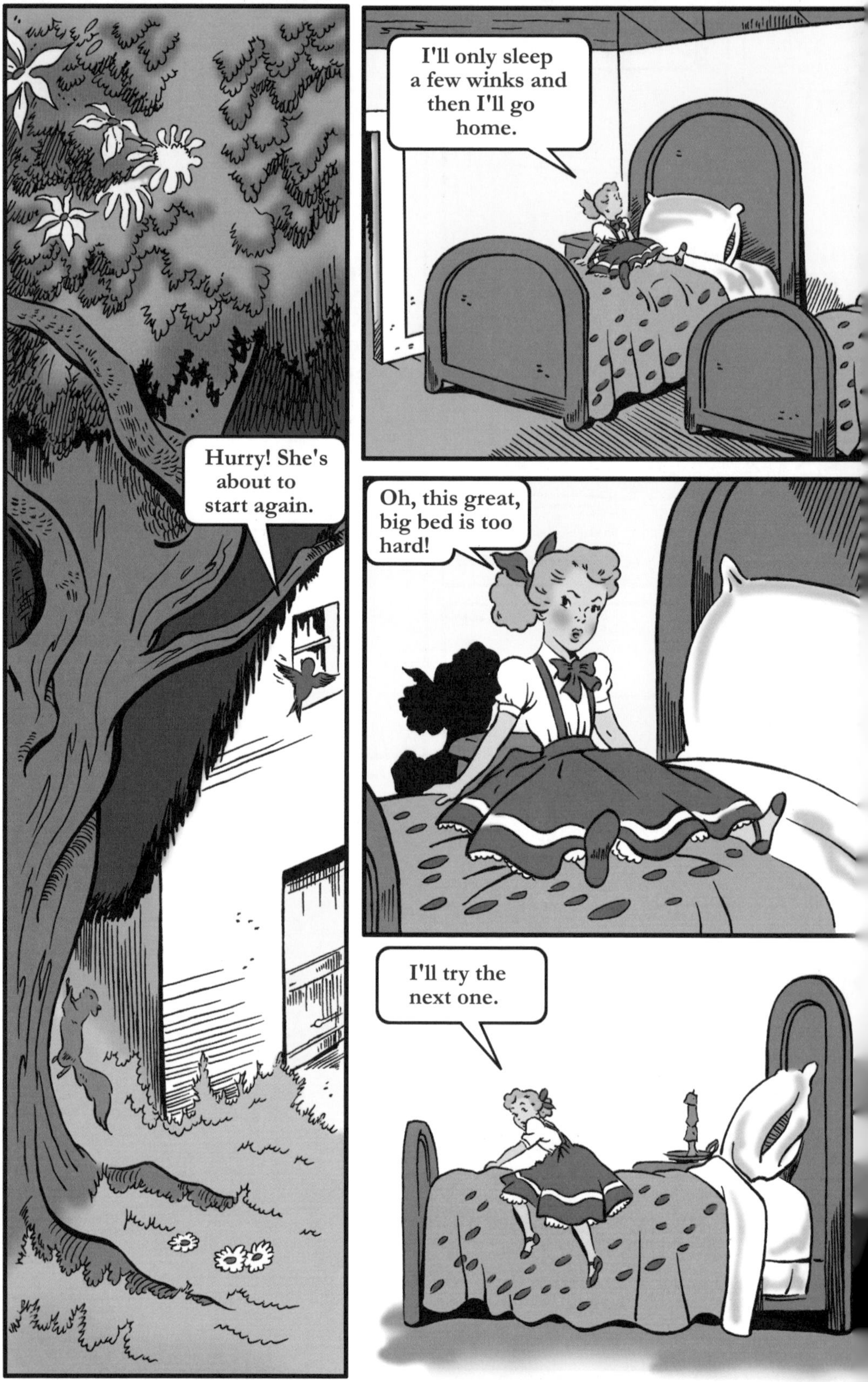
Hurry! She's about to start again.
I'll only sleep a few winks and then I'll go home.
Oh, this great, big bed is too hard!
I'll try the next one.

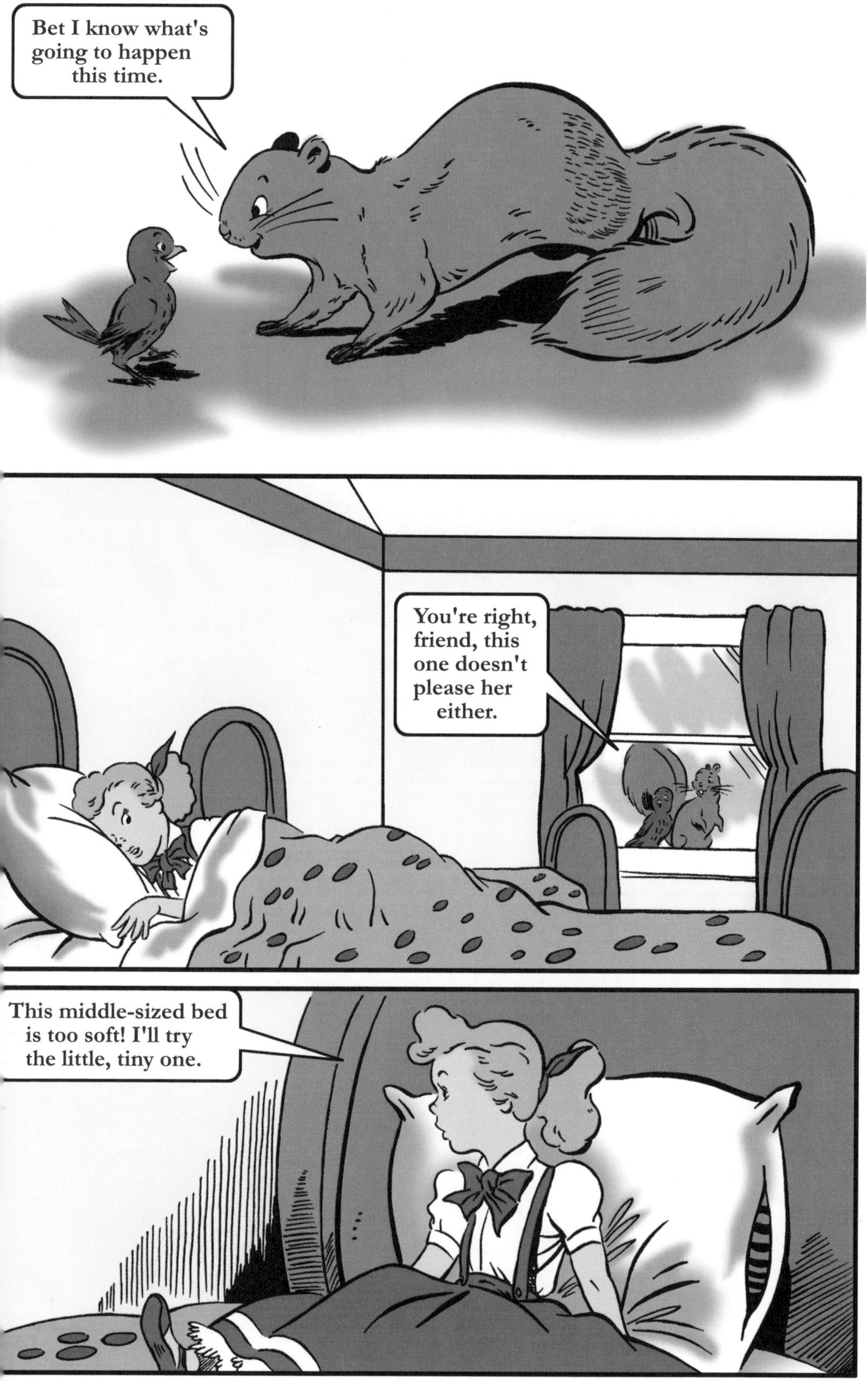
Bet I know what's going to happen this time.
You're right, friend, this one doesn't please her either.
This middle-sized bed is too soft! I'll try the little, tiny one.

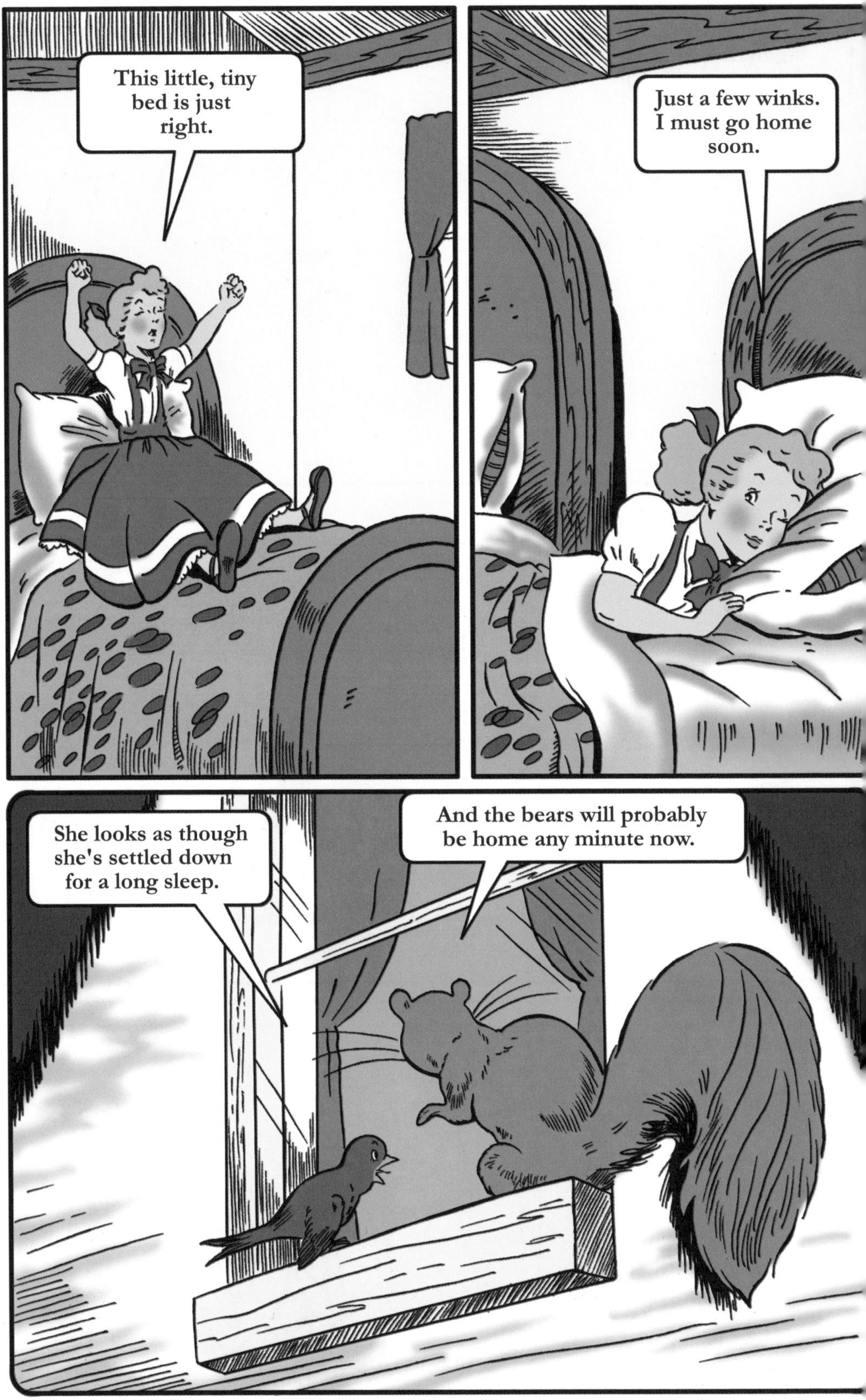
This little, tiny bed is just right.
Just a few winks. I must go home soon.
She looks as though she's settled down for a long sleep.
And the bears will probably be home any minute now.

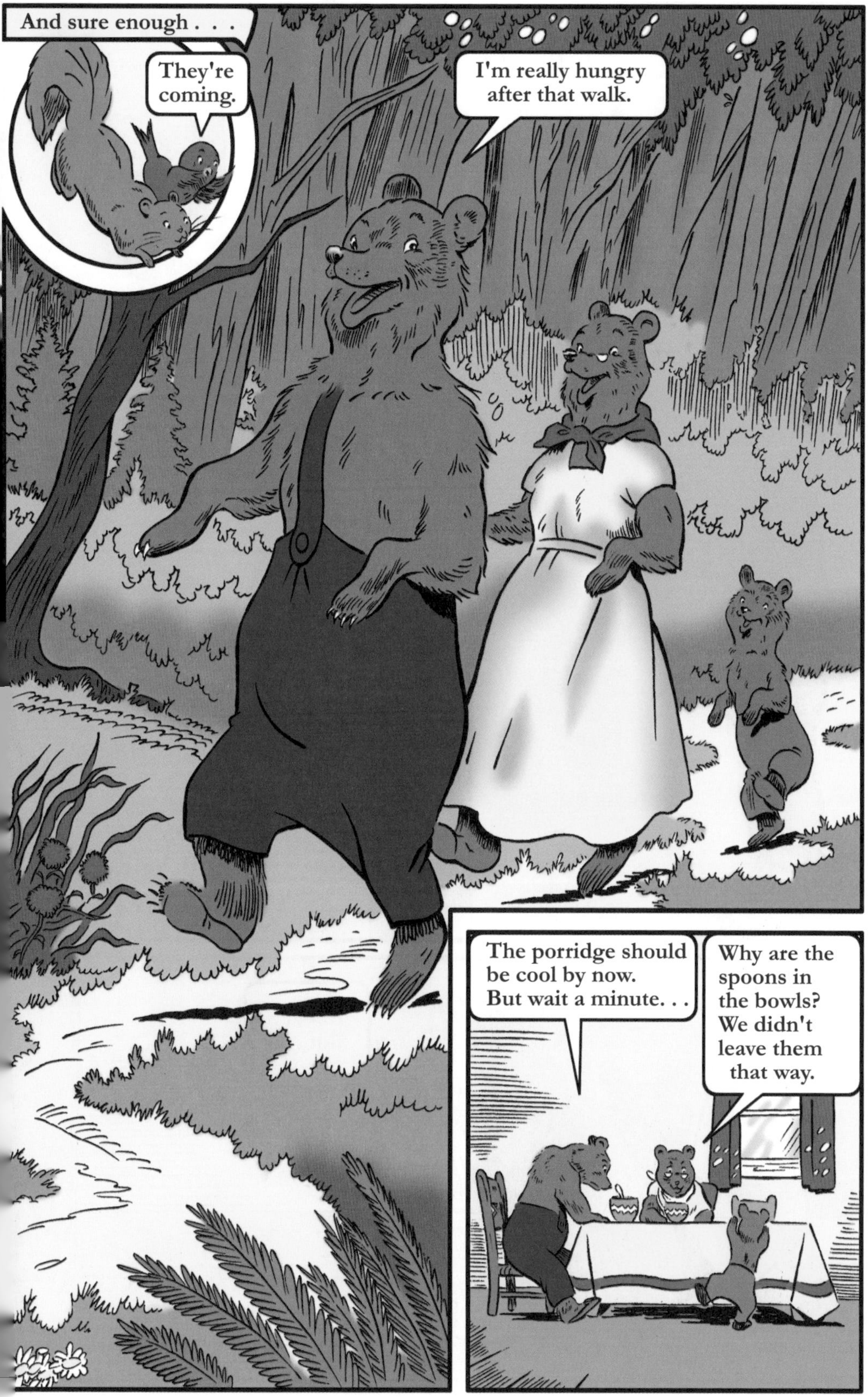
And sure enough . . .
They're coming.
I'm really hungry after that walk.
The porridge should be cool by now. But wait a minute. . .
Why are the spoons in the bowls? We didn't leave them that way.

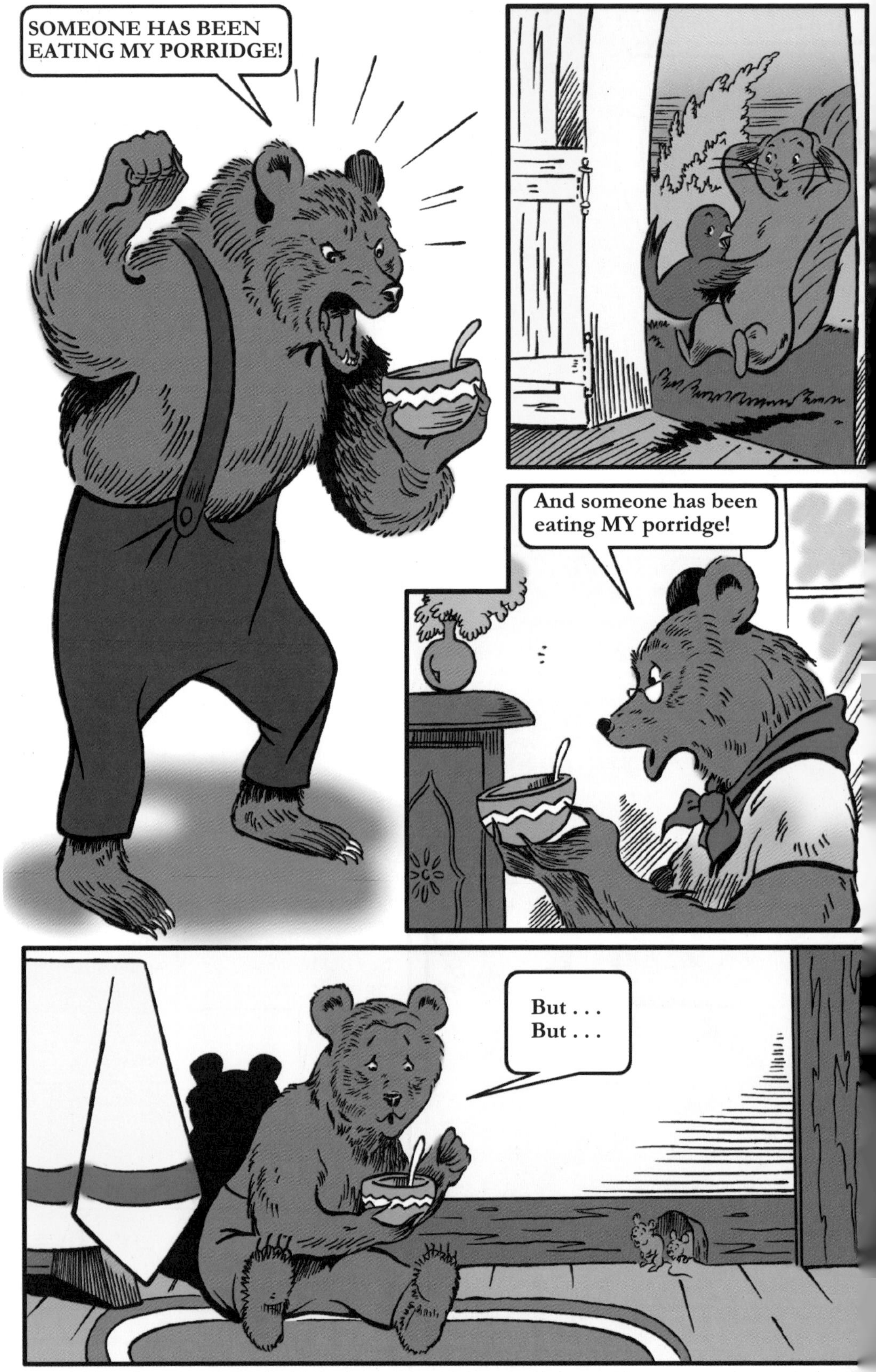
SOMEONE HAS BEEN EATING MY PORRIDGE!
And someone has been eating MY porridge!
But . . .
But . . .

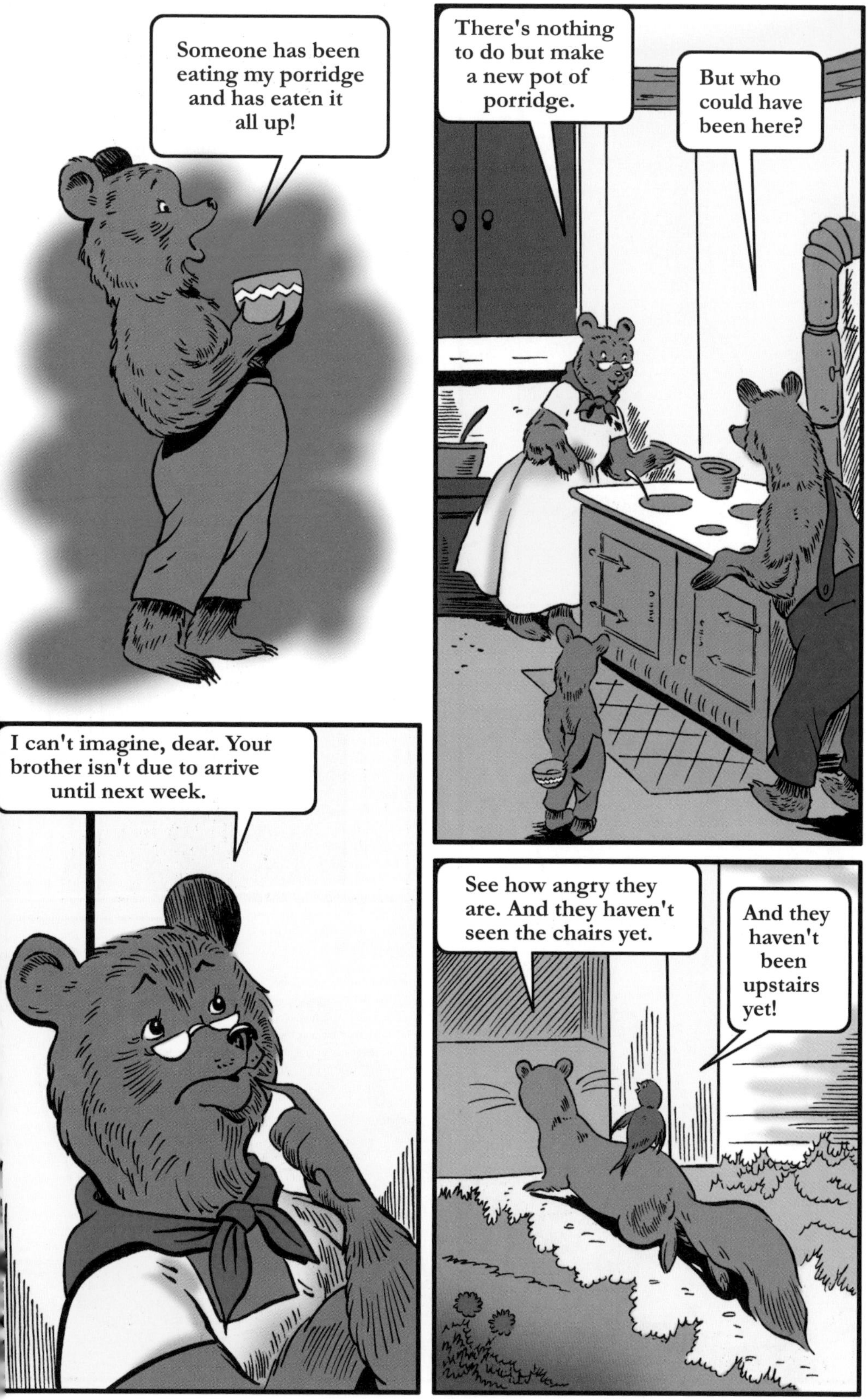
Someone has been eating my porridge and has eaten it all up!
There's nothing to do but make a new pot of porridge.
But who could have been here?
I can't imagine, dear. Your brother isn't due to arrive until next week.
See how angry they are. And they haven't seen the chairs yet.
And they haven't been upstairs yet!

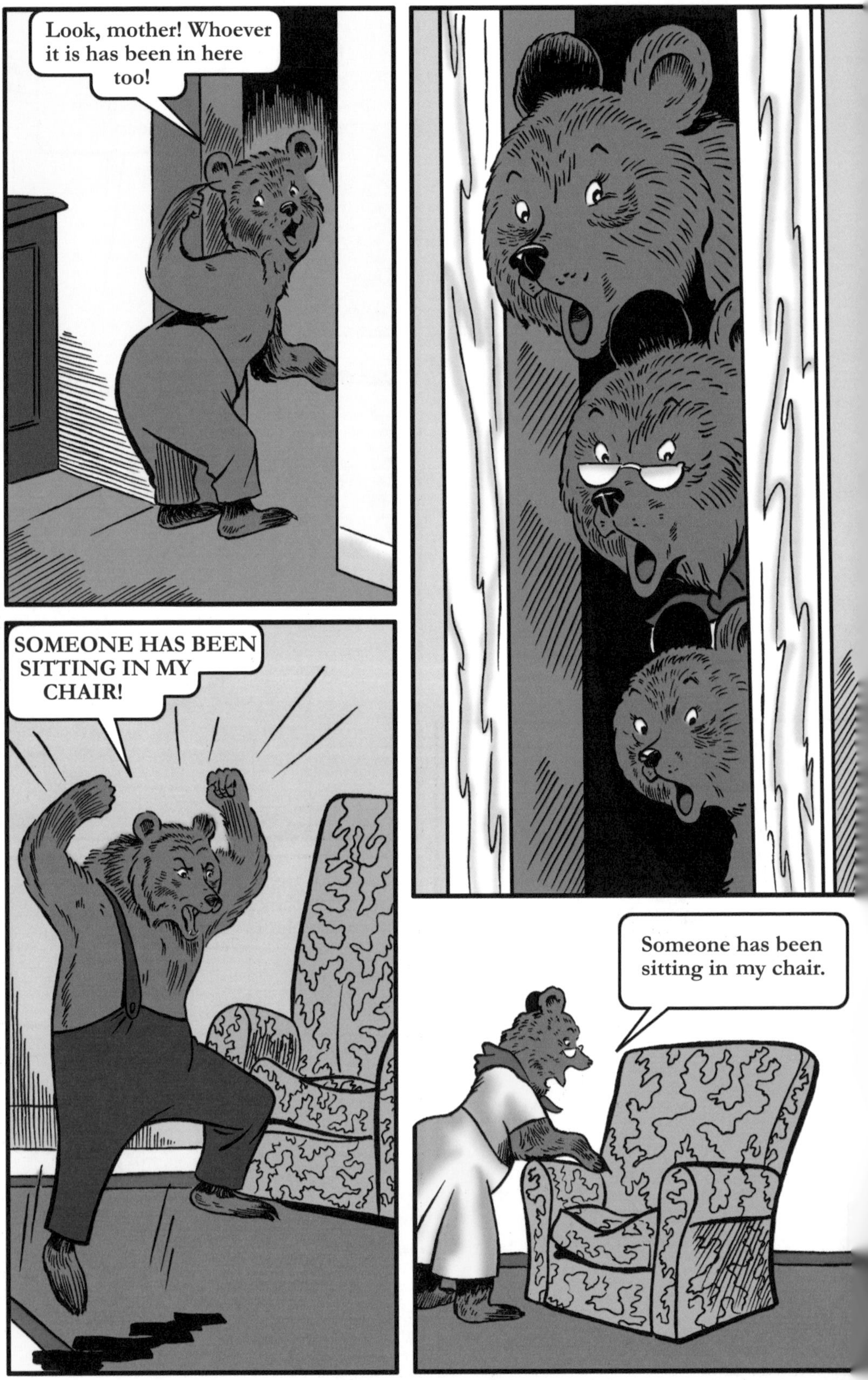
Look, mother! Whoever it is has been in here too!
SOMEONE HAS BEEN SITTING IN MY CHAIR!
Someone has been sitting in my chair.

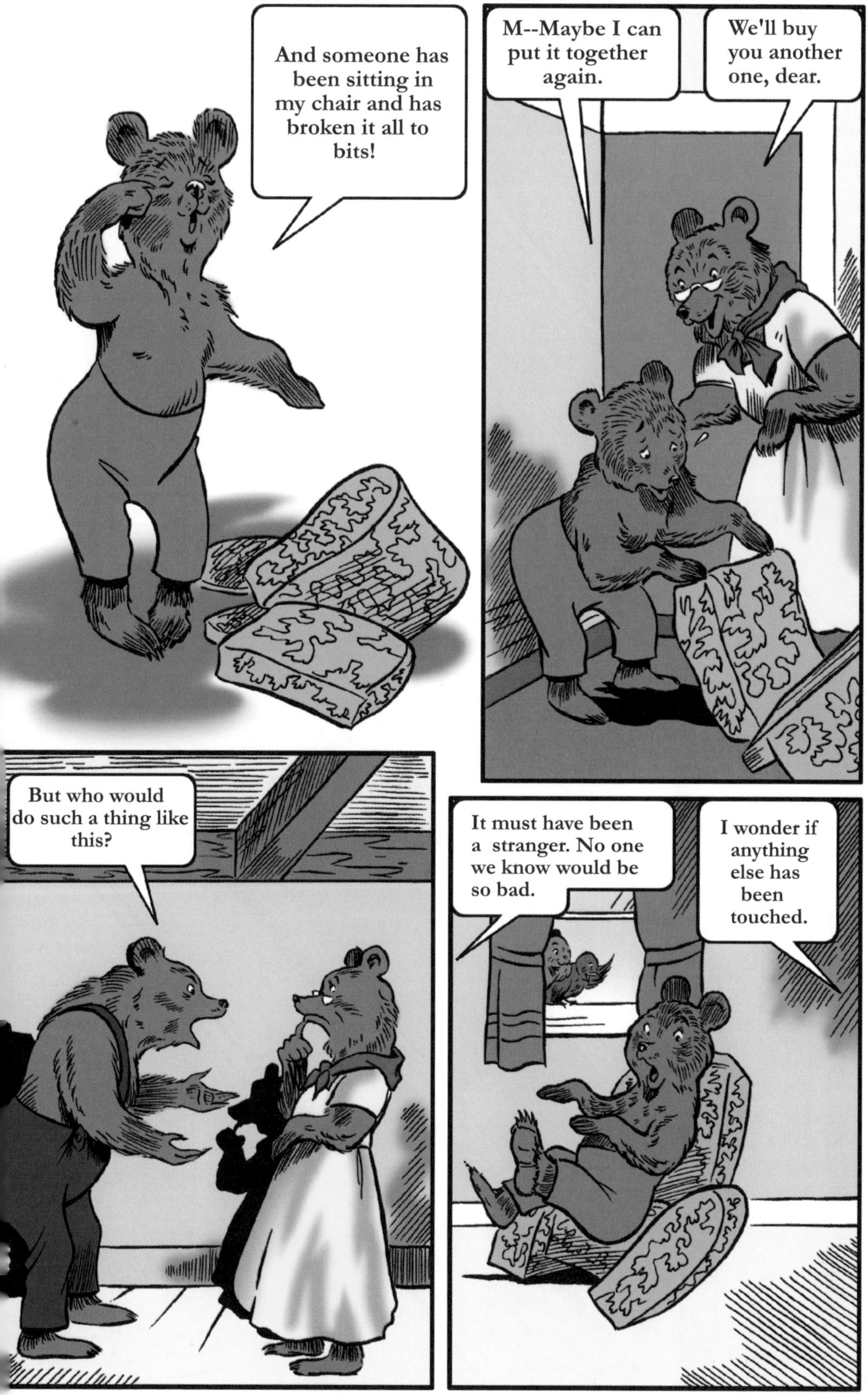
And someone has been sitting in my chair and has broken it all to bits!
M--Maybe I can put it together again.
We'll buy you another one, dear.
But who would do such a thing like this?
It must have been a stranger. No one we know would be so bad.
I wonder if anything else has been touched.

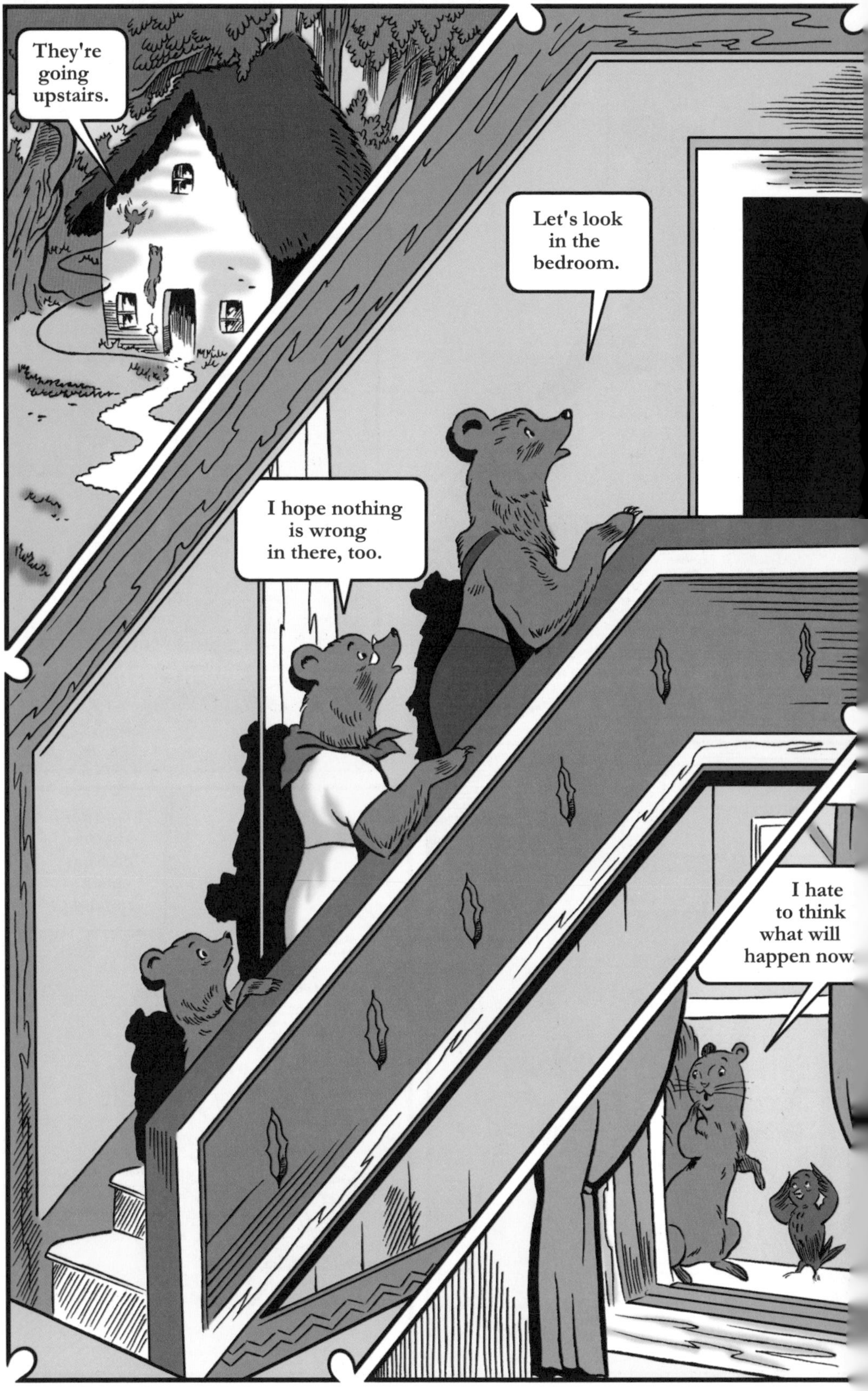
They're going upstairs.
Let's look in the bedroom.
I hope nothing is wrong in there, too.
I hate to think what will happen now.

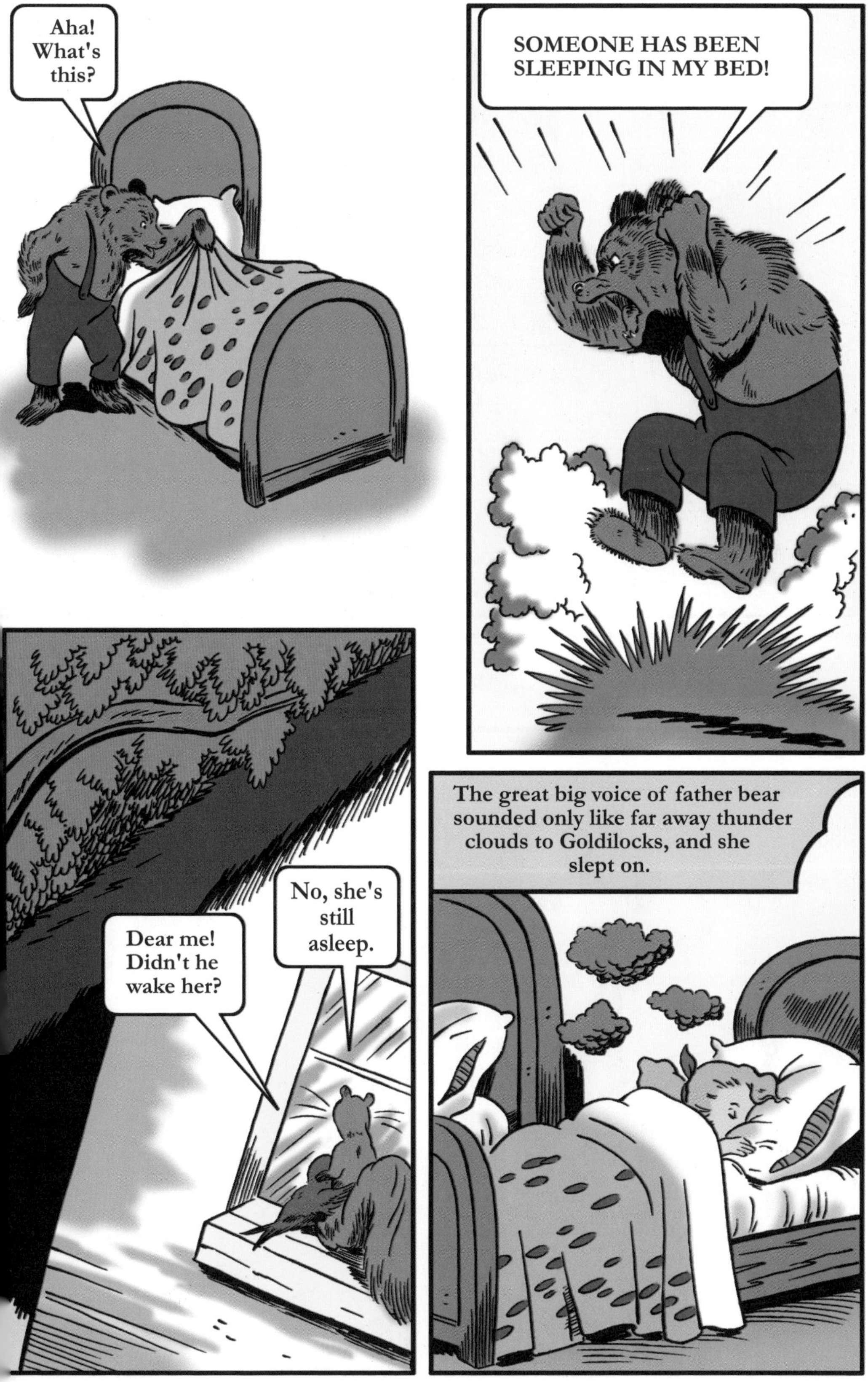
Aha! What's this?
SOMEONE HAS BEEN SLEEPING IN MY BED!
Dear me! Didn't he wake her?
No, she's still asleep.
The great big voice of father bear sounded only like far away thunder clouds to Goldilocks, and she slept on.

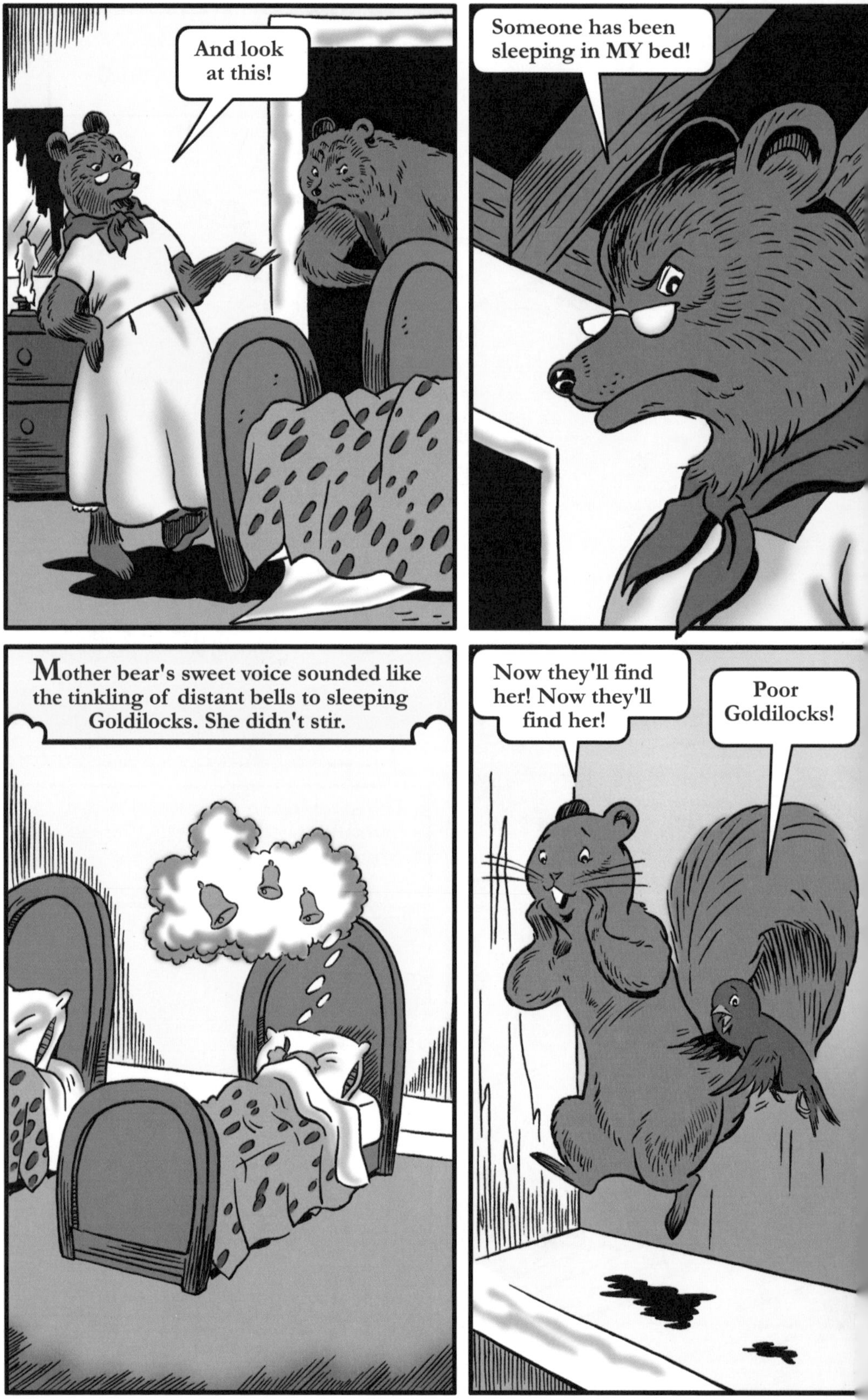
And look at this!
Someone has been sleeping in MY bed!
Mother bear's sweet voice sounded like the tinkling of distant bells to sleeping Goldilocks. She didn't stir.
Now they'll find her! Now they'll find her!
Poor Goldilocks!

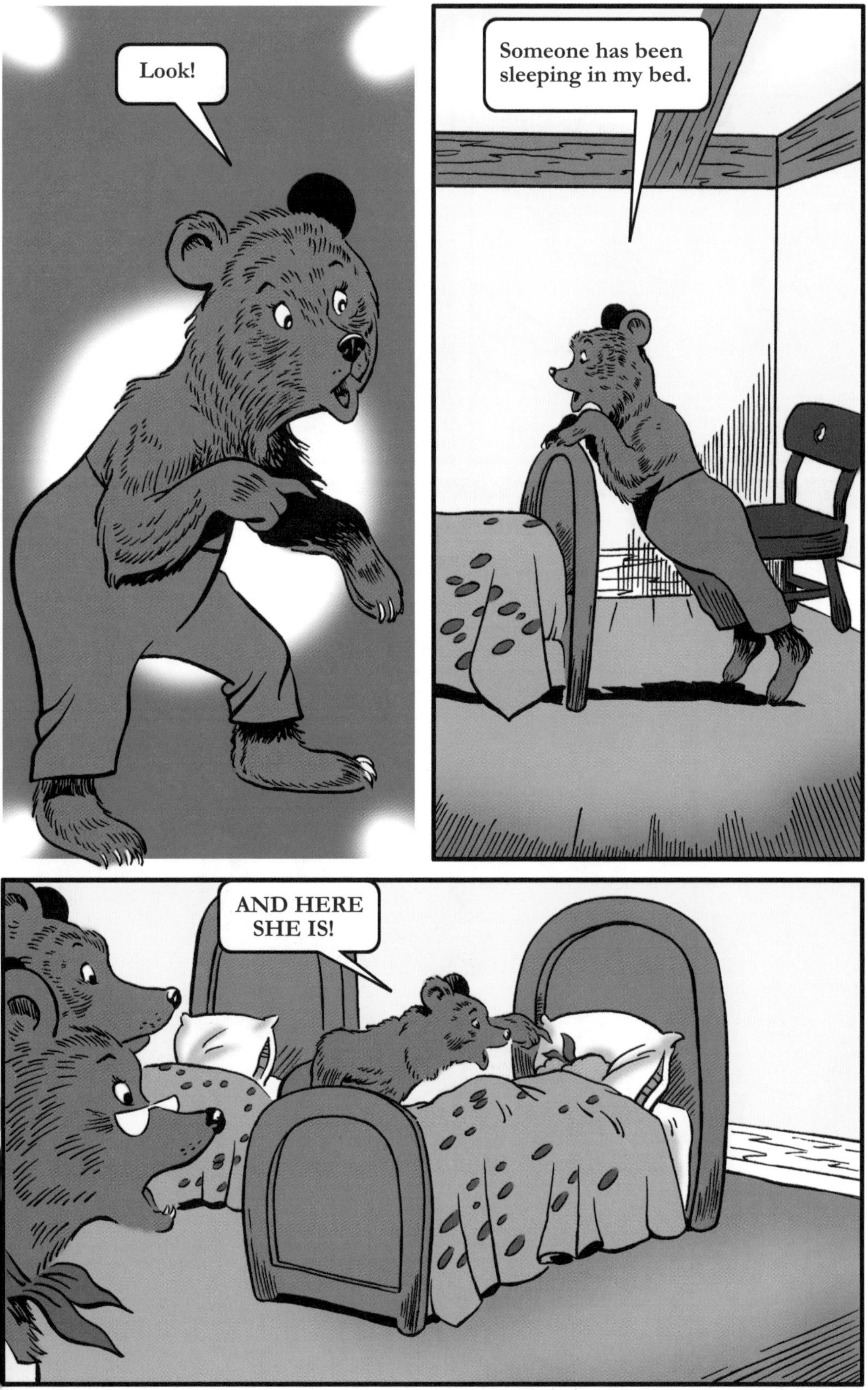
Look!
Someone has been sleeping in my bed.
AND HERE SHE IS!

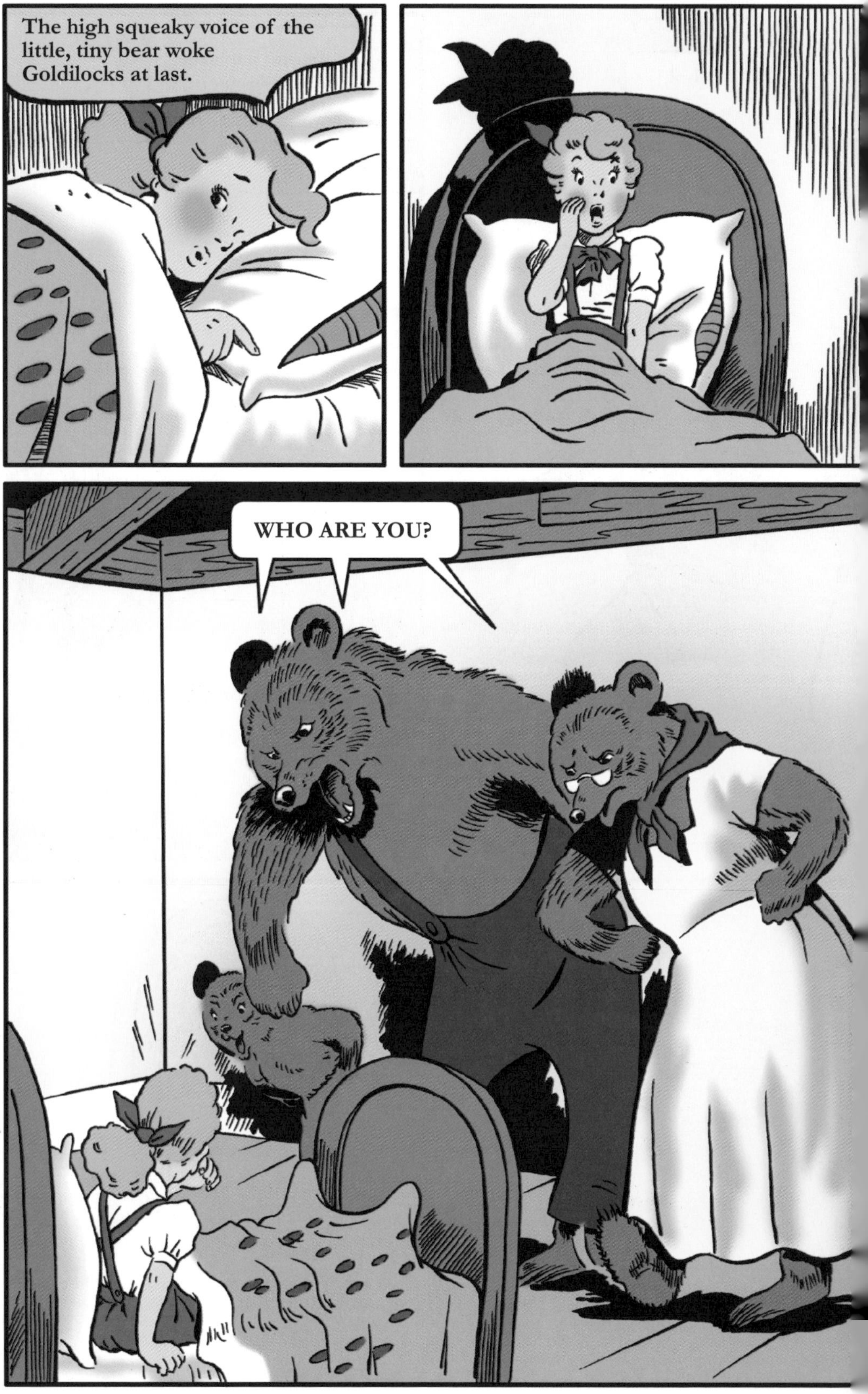
The high squeaky voice of the little, tiny bear woke Goldilocks at last.
WHO ARE YOU?

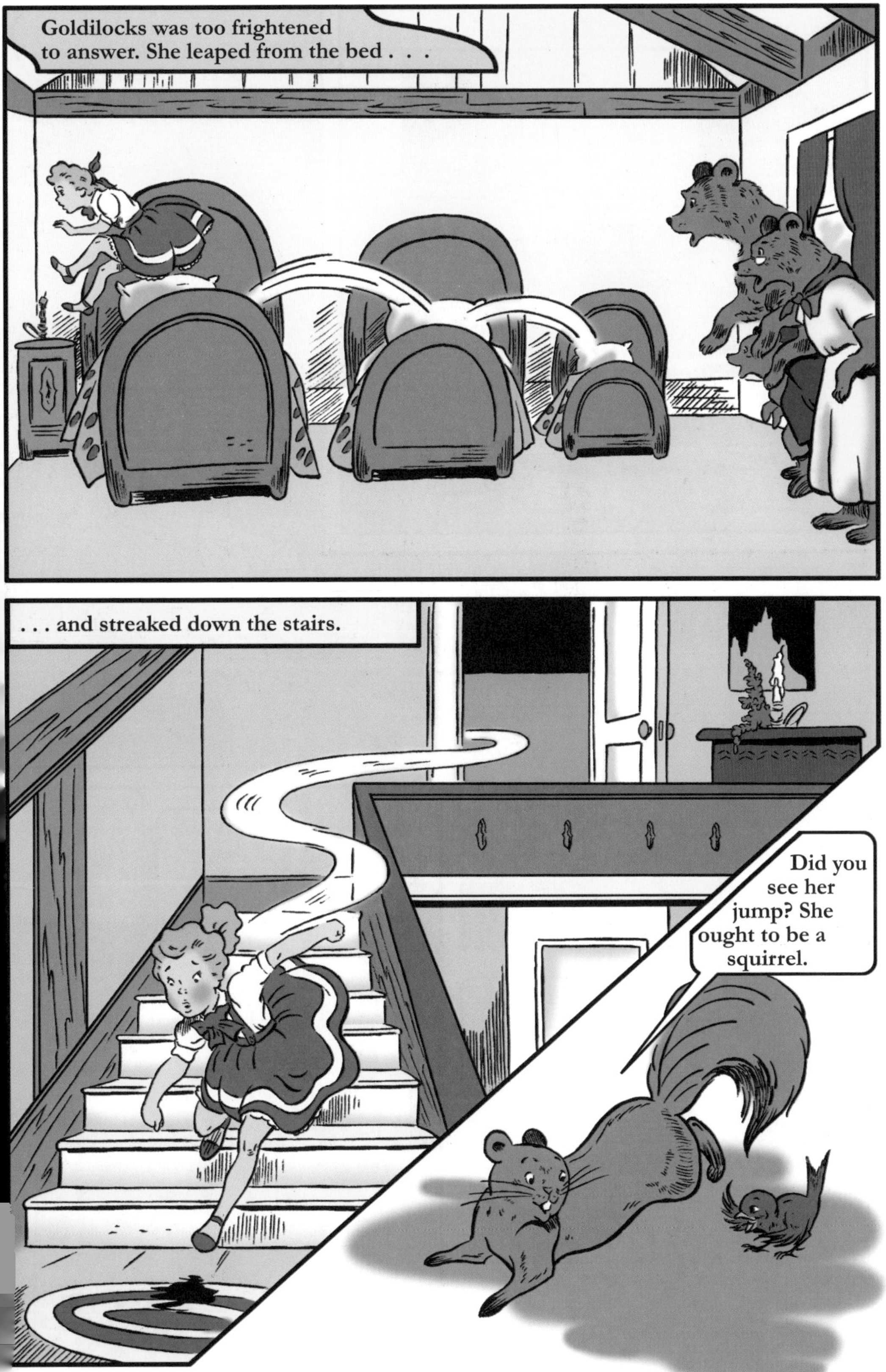
Goldilocks was too frightened to answer. She leaped from the bed . . .
. . . and streaked down the stairs.
Did you see her jump? She ought to be a squirrel.

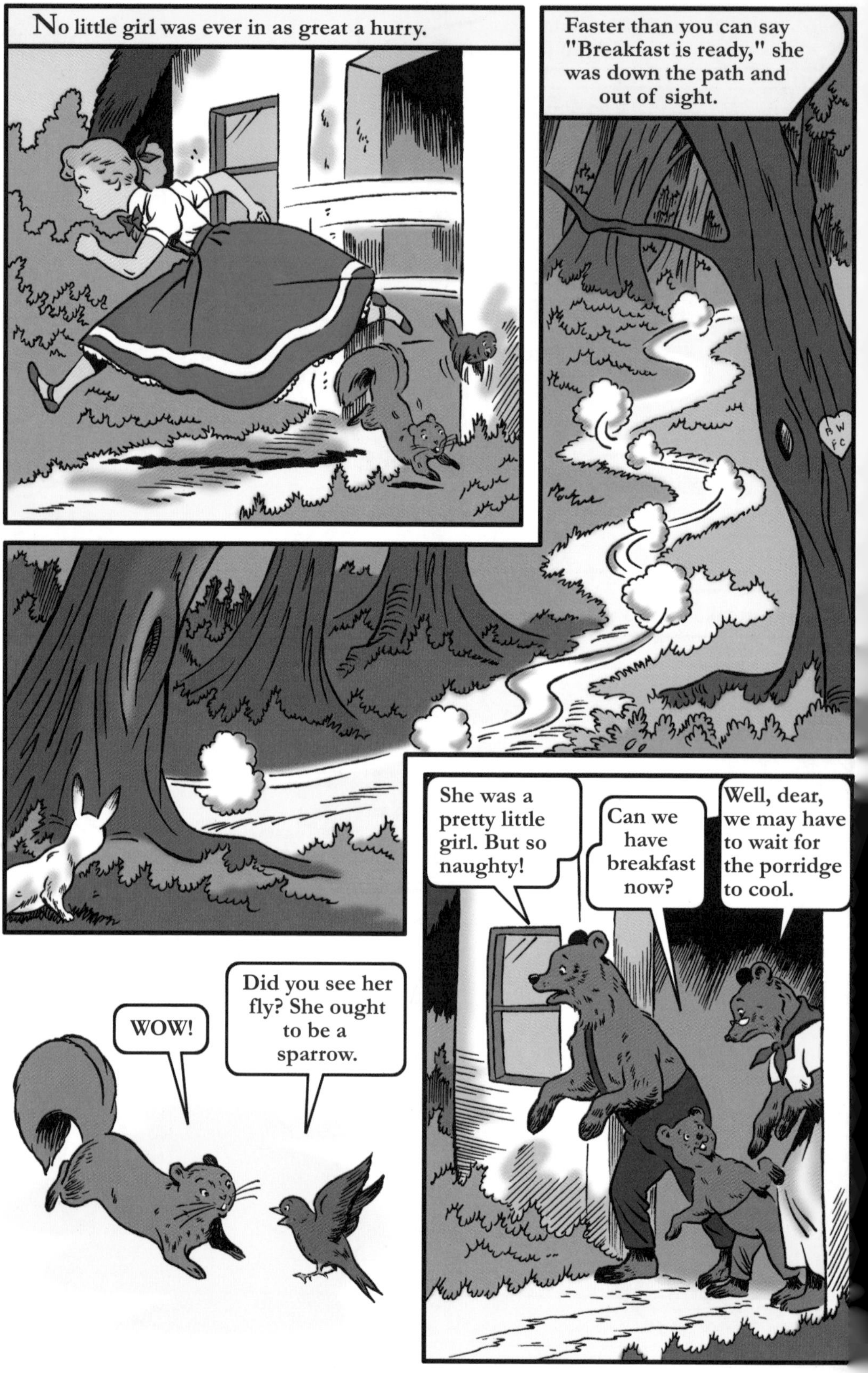
No little girl was ever in as great a hurry.
Faster than you can say "Breakfast is ready," she was down the path and out of sight.
WOW!
Did you see her fly? She ought to be a sparrow.
She was a pretty little girl. But so naughty!
Can we have breakfast now?
Well, dear, we may have to wait for the porridge to cool.

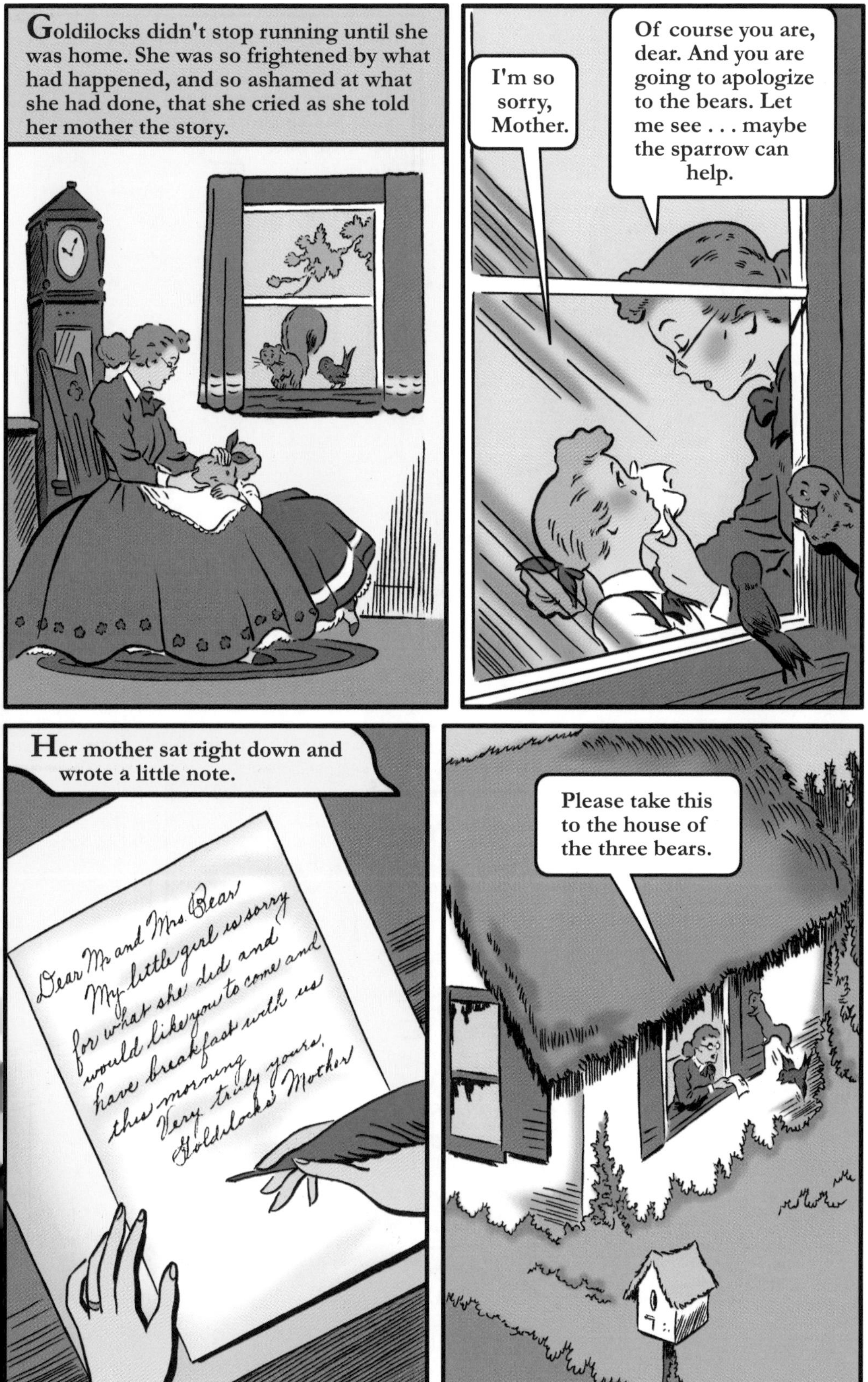
Goldilocks didn't stop running until she was home. She was so frightened by what had happened, and so ashamed at what she had done, that she cried as she told her mother the story.
I'm so sorry, Mother.
Of course you are, dear. And you are going to apologize to the bears. Let me see . . . maybe the sparrow can help.
Her mother sat right down and wrote a little note.
Dear Mr and Mrs. Bear
My little girl is sorry
for what she did and
would like you to come and
have breakfast with us
this morning
Very truly yours,
Goldilocks' Mother
Please take this to the house of the three bears.

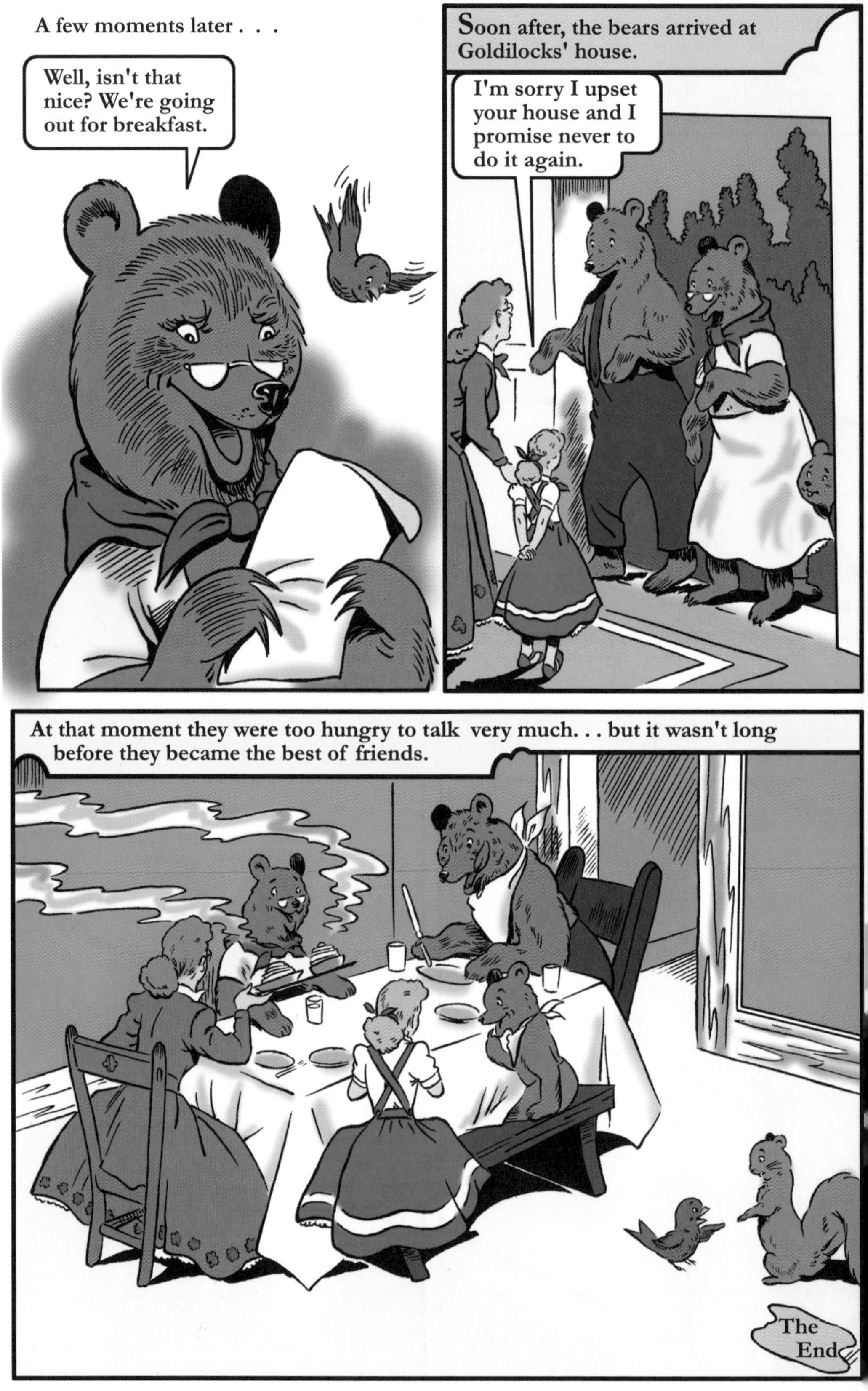
A few moments later . . .
Well, isn't that nice? We're going out for breakfast.
Soon after, the bears arrived at Goldilocks' house.
I'm sorry I upset your house and I promise never to do it again.
At that moment they were too hungry to talk very much. . . but it wasn't long before they became the best of friends.
The End

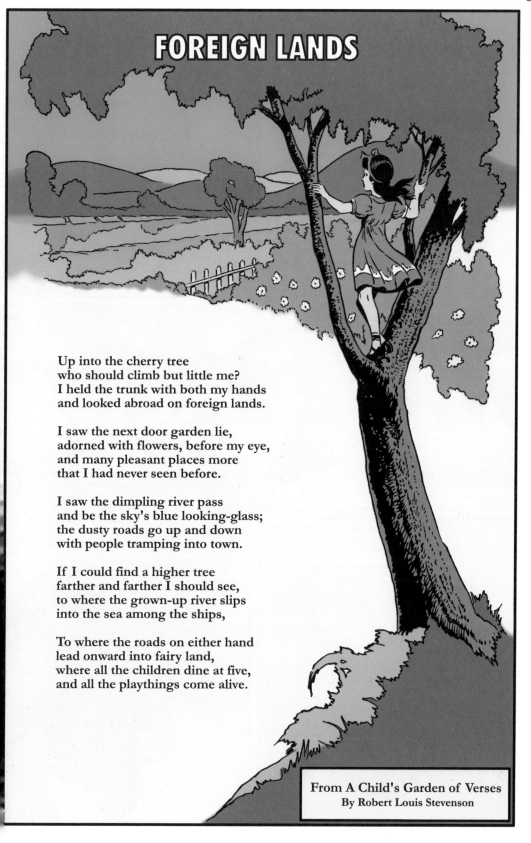

FOREIGN LANDS

Up into the cherry tree
who should climb but little me?
I held the trunk with both my hands
and looked abroad on foreign lands.

I saw the next door garden lie,
adorned with flowers, before my eye,
and many pleasant places more
that I had never seen before.

I saw the dimpling river pass
and be the sky's blue looking-glass;
the dusty roads go up and down
with people tramping into town.

If I could find a higher tree
farther and farther I should see,
to where the grown-up river slips
into the sea among the ships,

To where the roads on either hand
lead onward into fairy land,
where all the children dine at five,
and all the playthings come alive.

From A Child's Garden of Verses
By Robert Louis Stevenson

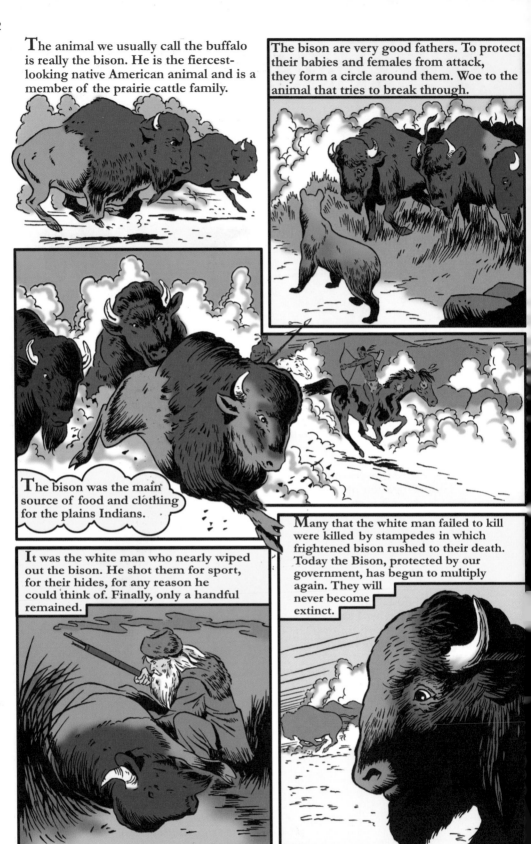

The animal we usually call the buffalo is really the bison. He is the fiercest-looking native American animal and is a member of the prairie cattle family.

The bison are very good fathers. To protect their babies and females from attack, they form a circle around them. Woe to the animal that tries to break through.

The bison was the main source of food and clothing for the plains Indians.

It was the white man who nearly wiped out the bison. He shot them for sport, for their hides, for any reason he could think of. Finally, only a handful remained.

Many that the white man failed to kill were killed by stampedes in which frightened bison rushed to their death. Today the Bison, protected by our government, has begun to multiply again. They will never become extinct.